CONVICT'S CAPTIVE

BOOK ONE

By

I0679675

PAUL BLADES

Other Books by Paul Blades:

CHAPTER ONE

The man was in Carly's car before she even knew it. She had filled up with regular at the self service pump with her debit card. It was a little after midnight and the station was deserted but for her old, beat up, maroon Malibu. The window of the convenience store was so filled with junk and advertisements that there was no way that the attendant could see out of it. She had been putting the card back in her wallet as she got back into the driver's seat. She had just closed the door when she felt an ominous presence next to her. She turned to her right and there he was.

He was large and gruff looking, and he seemed to Carly to be in his late forties. He was wearing a black knit cap and had a bulky, waist length coat on, colored light beige. His face was hard and thick, black whiskers covered it from his cheeks to his chin. He was wearing khaki pants and heavy, tan work boots. He had a sharp, long bladed knife in his hand.

"You know," he said to her in a gruff voice. "I'll bet I could slit your throat from ear to ear before you got even one step out of the car. You want to try it?"

A stark coldness came over her. Her belly roiled. Her hands, clasped on the steering wheel, started to shake. She felt her lips start to vibrate with the beginning of a sob and her eyes grew misty.

"Please don't hurt me," she said softly. "I'll let you have the car. I'll give you all my money."

"Shut the fuck up!" he said back angrily. "Just keep your mouth shut and drive the car. Take a right out of the station and head up the road. I'll tell you where to go."

"Pllllleeeeeease!" Carly whined. "Please let me go. I'll let you get away." Her voice was tremulous and her hands were shaking. She could feel her heart pounding in her chest. Her mouth had gone dry and a sickness was spreading all through her body.

The man's hand lashed out like lightning. She felt the blow, it seemed, even before she saw the fist strike her arm. It felt like someone had struck it with a sledgehammer.

"Owwwwwwwwwwwwww!" she screamed. "Ohhhhhh-hhhh! Oh, god, please don't hurt me! Pleeeeeeease!" Tears started to flow down her face. She had never been as scared in her life. Her left hand covered where she had been struck.

"I told you to shut the fuck up!" the man boomed at her. "Next time I'll just bury this about six inches into your ribs," he added menacingly, brandishing the fearful looking blade. "Get this piece of shit car going and start driving!"

Tears flowing down her face, Carly nodded and started the engine. It purred to life. Her boyfriend, Randy, kept it well tuned up. She had just left his place. They had gone out to dinner that night. Carly had gotten all spruced up for it, a bright yellow dress that came down to mid-thigh, yellow pumps, bright red lipstick. She had done her finger and toenails to match. It was their two year anniversary for when they started dating.

Afterwards, they had gone back to his apartment and made love. She had to go into to work extra early in the morning, so she decided against staying over. And she decided it was better to fill up her gas tank tonight rather than in the morning when she would be in a hurry. She hadn't expected anything like this to happen.

She gave the man a frightened look and pulled out north onto Route 29. There was hardly any traffic. The night was clear and a bright half moon lit the fields and woods to either side. Her right arm was aching terribly where the man had punched her. She knew that tomorrow it would be all black and blue. The russet colored parka that she wore hadn't had enough padding to soften the blow.

He told her to buckle her seat belt. She had left it off in case she got a chance to jump out of the car. Having the seat belt on would make it just that more difficult and give him more time to cut her with his vicious looking knife. She held the steering wheel with her left hand while she pulled the strap across her chest and buckled the seat belt in place. He put his on too, probably to guard against her stopping short and making him plow into the windshield. He was thinking of everything.

Route 29 was two laned here. Her headlights were reflected in the newly painted yellow lines the County had put in last summer. They had also installed little reflectors every fifty feet or so and they lit up like so many peering eyes as she began to whip by them. She had the speed up to forty five pretty quickly and then let it ease up to fifty. Her mind was racing with the possibilities inherent in this dreadful turn her life had taken. Maybe it was better that she should crash the car and make a run for it. The man looked like he was capable of anything. She said a quick prayer and tried to hold back her tears so that she could see the road clearly. Her eyes were focused straight ahead although she could see the man's bulk out of the corner of her right eye. He was leaning back and thumbing his knife.

They had gone about three miles when she got the courage to speak up. "Where are you taking me?" she asked plaintively.

Like sprung from a trap, the man's fist lashed out again. It struck her arm so hard that she almost drove right off the road.

"Owwwwwwwwwwwww! Ohhhhhhhhhhh! Ohhhhh-hhhhh!" she cried out. Tears began to stream down her face. She couldn't see. She pulled over and stopped the car and started to sob. She felt his hand take hold of her hair behind her head and pull her head back. The knife was at her throat. It pricked her skin.

"One more time, you stupid cunt, and I'll pull you out of this car, slit your throat and leave you by the side of the road!" he yelled. "I want you to keep your fucking mouth shut and drive. Do you understand? You'll find out where I'm taking you when we get there. And if you want to get there without your throat being slit, you better cooperate. Got it!"

"Yes! Yes!" Carly answered desperately. "I'll be quiet! I promise! Pleeeeeeeease don't hurt me anymore!"

He released her hair. There wasn't a whole lot to grab. Carly liked to keep her golden blond hair short, cut a few inches up from her shoulders. But there had been enough to make her feel that he was about to yank a skein of it right out of her head. Her right foot was jamming the break pedal down. When the man let go of her, she slowly let it up. She jammed it down again when a car came speeding up from behind them, the headlights illuminating the interior of her car, its horn wailing as it passed.

"Watch what your doing you stupid cunt!" the man spat out at her. Carly felt a grimace break out over her face. She could feel her body sweating. Her palms were slippery. Her heart was thumping madly and her arm, her right arm, was throbbing intently. She blinked her eyes to shake out the tears, looked in the rear view mirror and then eased up on the brake. They were back on the road.

They were going the direction Carly was going to take to get home to her place. It was about 8 or 9 miles up the road. When they passed her turnoff, on the left, a long dirt road with three mailboxes at the entrance, she gave out a little sob. She quickly looked over at the man to see if he was going to hit her again, but he hadn't noticed. A sinking feeling came over her and she pressed on.

Carly hadn't had the chance to put her wallet back in her handbag, a plump, yellow thing with a golden brass clasp. She sensed the man picking it up. She gave him a little glance and then fixed her eyes back on the road. It was her life he was holding in his hand, everything about her was in there: her license and employee i.d., her two credit cards, her debit card from Green Mountain Bank and Trust, pictures, mementos, an organ donor card, her four year old senior i.d. from Barrington High. Randy's picture. The man idly flipped through it. He pulled out the debit and credit cards and the $72.00 worth of cash she had in it, and then tossed the wallet back onto the console between the seats. He picked up her purse.

"You smoke?" he asked her calmly, as if they were on some kind of weird blind date together.

"N-no," Carly managed to whimper back.

"Too bad," the man returned as he fished through her purse. There wasn't much in thcrc. Some tampons, a hairbrush, a makeup kit. A comb. Her cell phone. A small box of condoms and a tube of lubricating gel. The man lifted the two latter items out of the purse. "You come all prepared, don't you?" he asked, amused.

Carly said nothing in reply. Her stomach gave another heave as one of the possibilities she had contemplated earlier seemed to enlarge into a probability.

He stuffed the sex aids back into the purse and fished around some more. There was a little tin in there, about two inches wide and four inches long. He opened it. There were four, thin, tightly rolled joints and a few roaches. The man laughed.

"I thought you said you didn't smoke," he chuckled. Carly said nothing. He closed the tin and put it back.

Then he took the cell phone out. He hit a button and it lit up. He stared at it. Then he looked at her.

"I saw on TV that they can track you wherever you go with this. Is that true?"

"I-I don't know," Carly answered. She hadn't thought of it until she saw it. Of course they could. As long as she had the cell phone, the police could track her when she didn't show up tomorrow. She wondered how long it would take before somebody called the police.

The man smiled at her. He lowered the passenger side window and tossed it out. "Just in case," he said, grinning.

He grin made Carly shiver with fear. They would never find her now. She wanted to cry again.

He remained silent for the next twenty minutes. Each time a car came at them from the other direction, she contemplated crashing head on into it. She visualized the airbags filling up and the car careening wildly off the road. Then she thought of herself all disfigured and maimed from the crash and the poor people in the other car. And then the man might not be hurt. He would kill her. But maybe it was better to be killed now rather than later after a night of torture and abuse. On the other hand, he might just use her and let her go. Or maybe she could escape. Or maybe the police would stop them.

That thought emboldened her. She gave he man a sidelong glance. He was staring straight ahead. Cops patrolled this road all night. It was the main drag all the way up to the city, about 75 miles away. She pushed the gas pedal down a little more and the car picked up a little speed, almost imperceptibly. Her eyes flicked to her right. The man hadn't noticed. After a few minutes, she increased the speed again. The car was approaching sixty. The speed limit was fifty. A little later, she increased it again to sixty five. And then to seventy. If a cop saw them now, he would stop them for sure.

All of a sudden, the man came alert. "What the fuck are you doing?" he blurted out. "Slow down, you stupid cunt! Just so you know, if a cop stops us, I'll kill you first before I kill him! Understand!"

Carly felt like her last chance at escape had vanished. She immediately eased up on the gas and the car slowed. It went down to forty.

"Don't be cute," the man said roughly. "Keep the speed at fifty five. Not too slow and not too fast. Or if you want, you can take the rest of the trip in the trunk. Would you prefer that?"

"N-no" Carly whined. "Please don't."

"Then no more fucking around," the man said. When Carly had the speed back up to fifty five, he leaned back in his seat once more.

Just before Halleyville, the speed reduced to 35 and then 25. The highway expanded to four lancs and there were a few traffic lights. Closed up stores lined the road on either side. Bright street lights illuminated the road-way. The light in front of them turned amber and then red. Carly brought the car to a stop. A shiny new, silver pick up truck came out of the road to their right and went in the opposite direction. Carly looked at the driver. He looked at her. And then he was gone. Carly felt another bout of crying coming on and she stifled it.

The man looked around. On the corner, on the other side of the road, was a Green Mountain Bank and Trust branch. When he saw it, he told Carly to put on her blinker and make a left. When the light turned green, he directed her into the parking lot.

They pulled up to the bank building. The ATM was inside the well lit, glass enclosed foyer.

"Turn off the car," the man told her.

She complied.

He took the keys from the ignition and took hold of her wounded arm. Carly flinched from the pain.

"Come out this side," he instructed her.

He opened his door and then used the button on the arm rest to lock the doors. He had been playing with the buttons there to see what they did. This way, when she took off her seat belt, she would have to unlock the door before she got out and ran, giving him a couple more seconds to dash around the car and recapture her. He got out and then leaned back in and pulled on her arm. She undid her seat belt and climbed over the console, lifting her right leg first high over the stick shift. Her skirt ran up her thigh almost all the way, revealing the tops of her light tan, sheer, self supporting stockings. She had gone all out for Randy tonight and she had made love to him with them on. She bit her lip, knowing that the man was watching. As best she could, she brought her other leg over and then slid over the passenger seat. He pulled her out of the car.

Without letting go of her arm, he led her to the door to the bank foyer. "How does this work?" he asked her.

She looked at him. "How could he not know that?" she asked herself. She hesitated in answering. He gripped her arm tighter and shook it.

"How do you open the door?" he asked impatiently.

"You slide the card through that slot," she answered him timidly. "Then the door will unlock for about fifteen seconds or so."

He handed her her debit card.

"Okay, do it," he said.

Carly used her left hand to swipe the card along the slot. There was a series of three beeps. The man pulled on the glass door to the foyer and it opened. He pulled her inside and over to the ATM.

He looked at it carefully, as if he had never seen one up close. "How does this work?" he asked.

"You stick the card into that slot and then pull it out. Then you enter your pin number."

"Do it," he replied.

Carly saw all of her meager savings going up in smoke. But she did what he said. She could see her reflection in the dimmed out screen. Hers and his. They made a strange couple. His black hair was scraggly where it escaped from under his cap and he towered over her 5'7" frame. He was dressed like a man on a work gang and she was dressed for a night on the town. She slid the card into the ATM slot and the screen came to life. Their images disappeared.

She suppressed a whine as she entered her numerical password. The screen asked her what she wanted to do.

"Savings," the man instructed.

Carly poked at that portion of the screen.

"Balance," the man stated.

Carly hit the little box for balance. A number popped up. She had $2,225.32 in her savings account.

"Take it all," he told her.

"I can't," she said plaintively. "It will only allow you $500 at a time."

"Shit," the man spat out. "Try it anyway," he told her.

Carly entered $2,225.32 on the screen and hit enter. A message came back confirming what she had told the man. "Shit," he said again. "Okay, take out $500."

Her heart sinking, Carly did as she was told. When the cash came out of the slot, the man grabbed it.

"Now do checking," he told her.

Carly brought her checking balance up on the screen. $845.67.

"Take out the max," the man instructed her.

She obeyed. He snatched that money too. Her heart sank as she thought of all the checks that were going to bounce.

The man pulled from his pocket her Visa card. "Stick this in," he told her.

Carly despaired at the thought of the man raiding her credit card as well. She wondered whether the credit card company would give the money back when they found out how it was taken. But then, she thought, "I probably won't be alive anyway."

She slid the card in and a screen came up. She didn't wait for his instruction and she entered her pin number. She entered the cash advance request for $500.00 just like her debit card. That money also disappeared into the man's pocket. Finally, he had her Discover card and he raided that one too.

As they were preparing to go, the man looked up at the round object above the ATM machine. He was holding on to her arm, the one he had bruised so callously earlier. It made Carly wince.

"Hold on," he said. "Is that a camera?"

Carly looked at the object. "Yes," she answered.

"Than everything that we just did is on film," the man stated.

"Yes," Carly responded.

"And these withdrawals, the bank will know where and when we did them?"

Despair flowed over Carly. She was hoping that the man would not think of that. "Yes," she answered despondently.

"We'll have to deal with that," the man said.

$2,000 richer, the man led Carly back to the car. She got in on his side, like she had got out. He made her buckle herself in before he got in. When he was sitting in the passenger seat beside her he gave her the keys. They drove off.

They continued up the road. The man was studying the map that Carly kept in the glove box. He had gone through the whole glove box, rifling through the nonsense she kept in there. There wasn't much of use in it. He did pocket her Swiss Army knife that she kept there for emergencies. There was also a small flashlight.

Using the flashlight, the man traced their route so far with his finger. Carly tried to glance over to see where he was taking her, but the way he kept the map angled away from her, she couldn't tell. He put it away after a while and settled back. When they had gone twenty or so miles, it had taken them over a half hour to cover that distance, they went through another semi built up area. The man spied a convenience store open on the left hand side of the road.

"Pull in there," he told her.

When they came to a stop, he turned to her, showing her the knife again. "You're coming in with me. If you give me any trouble, I'll stick you like a pig. Then I'll have to kill the clerk as well. You don't want that to happen, do you?"

Carly eyed the man nervously. "N-no," she replied.

He had had her pull into a parking slot where they couldn't be seen from inside the store. He made her get out his side again.

"Stay close to me," he told her.

The store was well lit. There was a young, gangly kid behind the counter and no one else in the store. He was reading a book. He gave them a slight nod when they entered and went back to his story.

The man dragged Carly around the store, holding on to her injured arm, ordering her to pick up this and that. She had picked up a plastic carrying basket at the door and obediently put the items into it. Peanut butter, bread, a few cans of canned stew, soup, some baked beans, chips, a liter of Pepsi, cookies, napkins, and assorted other items, including a can of French Roast Maxwell House coffee. She was unhappy when he told her to put a roll of duct tape into the bag as well as a coil of thin clothesline. When they had gathered their stuff, he led her to the counter. Before adding everything up, he asked the kid to get a carton of Marlboro's and a pack of lighters. He tossed in a collection of candy bars. He bought three hotdogs from the automatic grill and had Carly put mustard and chili on them. Carly was surprised when he added a small rubber ball from a display on the counter to their pile.

The store had a shelf full of bottles of alcohol behind the counter. The man asked the kid for a fifth of Jim Beam.

"I can't," the kid said. "It's after 10 o'clock."

The man smiled, took a twenty out of his pocket, and placed it on the counter. The kid looked at him and then up at the security camera. The twenty dollar bill won out and he slipped the fifth into one of the plastic bags. He had Carly pay for the merchandise with a credit card, take another $40.00 out of her account, and then carry their loot out to the car. She put the bags into the back seat at the man's instructions and then climbed back into the car. When the man was settled, she started the engine and got back on the road in the direction they were traveling.

When they got on the road, the man pulled a sweatshirt our from under his coat. He had apparently shoplifted it when no one was looking. How he did it without her seeing it was perplexing. Why he did it was a conundrum. It wasn't his money they were spending. As he removed his outer jacket, Carly understood why he had lifted the sweatshirt. The man was obviously on the run from something. His beige jacket stood out like a sore thumb. He had taken the sweatshirt to disguise his appearance. He had not paid for it so that if the kid at the store was ever questioned, he would not be able to report what he would now be wearing. The man apparently had a finely honed craftiness. He would be a tough man to fool.

Underneath the jacket, he was wearing a white t-shirt. It looked new and remarkably white as if washed in bleach. Where the man came from and where they were going was a mystery. Had he committed a pernicious crime? Had he escaped from somewhere?

Then it struck her. He had escaped from prison. She had seen prison clothes before once when she had gone to the county courthouse for jury duty. Some the prisoners were picking up trash and manicuring the lawn and bushes. They had worn clothing just like the man was wearing.

She watched from the side of her eyes him putting on the sweat shirt. He was heavily muscled, like he had been working out for years. There was a tattoo on his neck, crudely drawn. It was some kind of Chinese or Japanese ideogram. There were some more tattoos on his arms. They looked like they had been drawn by a child. They were prison tattoos. She had heard about them. He slipped the sweatshirt over his head and down his torso. It was dark blue and had a white Michigan State logo on the front. He tossed his jacket into the back seat. He had also lifted a black baseball cap. He took off the knit cap that he had been wearing, tossed it back with the jacket and put the baseball cap on. He looked at her and smiled. "Presto, chango!" he said.

The man wolfed down the chili dogs, throwing the wrappers out the window as soon as he was done. He then ripped open the carton of cigarettes, opened a pack and lit one up. He gave a deep sigh as he released the initial intake of tar and nicotine. He looked at Carly. "Twelve years," he said. "It still feels just as good."

Twelve years since he had a cigarette. He had been in prison for twelve years! And if he had escaped after all that time, he must have had a long time left on his sentence. Otherwise it wouldn't make sense to escape. That meant that he had done something very, very bad.

The cigarette smoke filled up the passenger compartment. Carly hated cigarette smoke. Her father had died of lung cancer and she was of the opinion that all cigarettes should be outlawed and that anyone who smoked was stupid. She couldn't help but wish her father's fate on her kidnapper.

About ten minutes after they had left the store, the man ordered Carly to enter a shopping center parking lot and turn around. All the stores were closed and there were no other cars in the lot. He ordered Carly to get back on the road but in the other direction. Carla was perplexed. Were they going back to the store? They passed it about ten minutes later. She kept wondering what they were doing. After about another fifteen minutes they came to a crossroads. County Road 597 intersected Route 29. He told her to take a right.

Then she realized what was up. She had wondered about the use of the credit card. He knew that it could be traced. But by doubling back, he could deceive any pursuers into believing that he had continued to go north from the convenience store. If the kid was questioned, and if he noticed them leaving, he would tell the police that they had made a left out of the parking lot, going north. That's where they would look for them. Not here on Route 597 going west. A feeling of torpor passed through her as she resigned herself to her fate. Although she was sure that the man would be caught sooner or later, for her sake, it would certainly be later and, in all probability, much too late.

They drove through the night. The man made himself a peanut butter sandwich. He had bought a half gallon of milk and he drank it right from the carton. He lit up a new cigarette about every twenty minutes or so like he had never quit. He otherwise remained silent. He kept the radio off. She had wondered about that too, but now she knew that he didn't want her to have too much information about him. His escape must be all over the radio. She didn't even know his name.

The moon had sunk below the horizon and the night had turned dark. There were few lights along the winding, two laned country road they were following, limited to the occasional intersection with another County Road from time to time. Where Carly lived, the terrain was mostly flat, farming country, but to the west it became more hilly, as the land built up to the mountains beyond. There were hardly any other cars on the road. When one came towards them, Carly had the momentary illusion that the driver, whoever he or she was, would recognize her, and him, and call the police. But of course the vehicles were going too fast for any recognition to be possible. The glare of the headlights obscured the windshields of each of the cars, and as of yet, no one would know that she was missing.

Once in a while, a car would approach them from behind. Its headlights would illuminate the inside of the car. It would either follow them for fifteen or twenty minutes or so, and then pull off to one of the side roads, or rev up its engines and stream past them on some straightaway. Every time Carly saw the headlights approaching from the rear, she said a little prayer that it was a cop car and that the cop would find a reason to pull them over, but it never happened.

The man sat quietly, smoking cigarettes, eating cookies and chips, drinking from the half gallon of milk, or just staring into the windshield. The only sound was the slight noise of the well tuned engine and the hum of her radial tires on the pavement. He was completely self possessed, as if he had years and years of practice sitting alone and being his own, silent company. He had no interest in or need for chit chat. He didn't even put on the radio, which would have helped Carly maintain her alertness.

Ghostly looking, darkened, old houses swept past them, an occasional two pump gas station, a darkened diner or country store. Even the infrequent bar they passed was closed. Carly was becoming more and more tired as the night wore on. She found herself fading. He offered her some soda, but she declined. Once, he let her stop and pee by the side of the road. He made her woefully self conscious as he watched her draw her panties to her ankles from under her dress, spread her legs and release her water onto the road's apron. She thought of running off, but he was too close to her and poised, cat like, as if he expected her to give it a try. He made her sit in the car on the passenger side when he took his leak. She could not help but think of his cock in his hand and where it might be later.

The light on the dashboard said it was 4:45 when Carly began to fall asleep. She had left Randy's a little after 11:30. The man had kidnapped her about a half hour later. That meant that they had been driving for almost 5 hours. Three times she caught herself nodding off. The car would sway and she would realize that her eyes were closing and that her chin was sinking. After the third time, she finally told the man that she couldn't drive any more. She was too tired.

"Just a little further," he told her. "We'll find a place to stop."

A half hour later, they approached a motel on the right hand side. It consisted of a frame house that doubled as an office and a series of little cabins. The vacancy sign was on. He ordered her to pull into the lot.

When they got out of the car, they had to ring a bell to call down the night attendant. It took several long rings over a number of minutes. While the vacancy light had been on, all the inside lights were off. Finally, a light flicked on way back in the house. A few moments later, one flicked on in the office. A thin, elderly man came to the door. Carly could just make him out through the curtain that covered the inside of the window on the door. He fiddled with the door handle and then opened the door inwards.

The man had shown Carly the knife just before they rang the bell with the usual dreadful warning. He had told her what to say when they got inside.

"Hello! Hello!" the old man proclaimed. He was wearing a pair of striped pajamas and a thin cotton bathrobe, plaid with thin black lines on a field of red. His hair was mussy and gray, a little longer than short. He had a thin, boney nose and big ears. He was a little taller than Carly, but not taller than her kidnapper.

"You'll be wanting a room, I guess," the man said to them. "But I guess that's a stupid question this time of night. Come in! Come in! Latecomers are welcome! The wife says we ought to turn the light out at 11, but every once in a while we get a late customer like you two. Every little bit helps, you know."

He stepped behind a tall desk that was more like a free standing counter. It was covered with Formica, pink with black speckles. On it was a large light green pad with the black registration book open on it. A standing card listed their rates. Behind the desk was a large Currier and Ives print of some country scene. On the walls of the small room were prints of ducks and deer and other wildlife. The motel license hung in a frame and there was a sign that said that checkout time was 10 A.M., the letters burnt into a foot long piece of raw wood.

"How long ya staying?" the old man asked. He was looking at them, measuring them. Carly wore no ring and there was an obvious age difference between her and her captor, not to mention how they were dressed. She was nervous, wanting desperately to tell the man that she was a prisoner, and not wanting to provoke the carnage that would inevitably result if she did. She said the words she had been told.

"We'd like to stay the day. We've been traveling all night."

"Well, check out time is 10," the old man said. "If you want to stay longer you'll have to pay for two days."

"That's not a problem," Carly replied. There was a definite tremor in her voice, one she couldn't control. Her hands were shaking and she was afraid that the old man might notice it when she signed the register.

"That'll be $45 a day. $90 all told. Plus tax."

The man counted out five twenties and laid them on the desk. The old man scooped the bills up, put them in the drawer under the desk, and produced their change.

"You gotta sign the book," he said. And then looking them over again said, "It don't matter to me what name you use."

The man had told her what names to use. She signed the book Ralph and Alice Kramden. The old man looked at the names without comment.

He went to the rack on the wall behind the desk to select a key.

"We'd like one as far away from the road as possible," she told him. "We'll probably sleep most of the day and we don't want to be disturbed."

"I'll give ya number twelve, it's way in the back. Nice cabin too. Roomy, ya know. I usually get more for it, but as you paid for two days, I'll let it go," he announced. "There's color TV, cable, and the heat's good. We just redid the bathroom so it's real nice. You want I should show it to you?"

"No thanks," Carly answered. "We'll find it."

They had parked the car off to the side so that the motel clerk wouldn't see it. The man made Carly get in like before and they drove slowly deeper into the collection of huts. There were a few cars parked outside a few of the units and a long tractor trailer along the edge of the property. The numbers of the cabins were highlighted on their doors in brass lettering. They saw 10, then 11 and then 12, just like the man said, way in the back and about 30 yards away from the nearest cabin. The parking spot was partly obscured by a large evergreen tree. It was perfect for the man's needs.

He had her get out the passenger side and take all the bags out of the back seat. He held her arm and marched her to the door. She waited, her tiredness muting somewhat her terror of what awaited her beyond it. He hadn't touched her so far, at least not in that way, and he hadn't made any comments. "Maybe he's gay," she thought hopefully. She had heard that men did that in prison. Maybe he would leave her alone. And maybe, just maybe, when he fell asleep, she could escape.

The door swung inwards and the man motioned her to go in. It was all dark inside. He flicked the switch near the door, on the left. The room erupted in light. It was paneled in golden stained oak. There was a thin commercial carpet on the floor. The bed was a double, smaller than queen size. It was covered by a light green blanket. A brown and red comforter was folded at its foot. The foot of the bed faced the door. True to the old man's word, it seemed larger than the other cabins. There were two wooden chairs, stained to match the walls, abutting a small wooden table to the left of the bed.

A small refrigerator, about 2' by 3', sat next to a tiny sink and a two burner electric stove. An ashtray and two glasses covered with thin, white paper bags were on the table. The bathroom was on the other side. The TV was to the right of the door. It had a cable box. To the left of the door was a double window. The curtain was open. Under the window was an electric heater built into the wall. The room smelled a little musty as if there hadn't been anyone in it for a while.

All of a sudden a profound coldness came over Carly's body. It was maybe 25 degrees outside, but the heater in her car worked really well and she had been warm all night except when the man cracked his window when he smoked. The inside of the cabin was about the same temperature as outside. She could see her breath. Her knees felt weak and her stomach was queasy. The bed loomed large in front of her. What would he make her do there, she thought unhappily. She started to cry.

"Put those bags on the table," the man told her.

While she was doing that, he closed the curtain to the large window and turned on the wall heater. It roared to life and hot air started to stream out of it.

"Go sit over there," the man told her, pointing to the other side of the bed near the bathroom.

Carly, obediently and morosely, shuffled over to the bed and sat down. She had to turn her body so that she could keep her eyes on the man.

He sat down in one of the chairs. Then he seemed to think a minute. He got up and said, "Stay right there," and walked out the door.

Carly's heart started to race. She was all alone! She looked quickly around. There was a window just opposite the bed, no more than three feet away from her. It was locked, but all it needed was a twist of the clasp at the top of the bottom half. She could be out in a second! She would run, run, run! She would scream! She would get away!

But what if he caught her? What would he do? He would slice her up! He would kill her! But maybe not! Maybe she would get away! Maybe he would hop in the car and make a getaway before anyone came out of the other cabins! She had to try it! She just had to!

Just as she was getting up the nerve to rise and approach the window, the door to the cabin opened again. He had in his arms the jacket and cap he had been wearing and her yellow purse. If anyone came up to the car while they were sleeping, they wouldn't see them now. He was careful all right.

Despair flowed through Carly's body like a sickness. She was a fool! Her indecision has cost her her chance, maybe her life! Why was she such a coward? She thought she was going to throw up.

The man tossed the purse on the bed and the jacket and knit cap onto the floor by the wall and regained his seat in the chair. He took off the black baseball cap and tossed it away. He pulled the sweat shirt off of his torso and tossed it over by the jacket and cap. He got up and did some more exploring of the little cabin. There was a narrow broom closet with an ironing board and a yellow straw broom. Over the stove was a small cabinet that held an old fashioned, four cup percolator coffee pot, some bowls and plates, some condiments and some more glasses and a couple of coffee cups.

Carly just sat on the bed, eyeing the man warily as he moved about. When he was done exploring, he came back to his chair and sat down. He leaned over, his hands on his knees. His white t-shirt was pulled tight over his chest. His arms were large and round. With his black beard and wild hair he looked a bit like a pirate. Blackbeard. He reminded her of Blackbeard. He was the terror of the high seas. He had pillaged and looted. He had no conscience and was cruel and ruthless. Carly shivered with fear.

"Okay," he said as his eyes peered into her, "it's warm enough now. Take off your clothes."

Carly grimaced. People said that she had a cute, pert look. Her nose was short, not too short or button like, but just the right size to complement her face. Her lips were thick, not too thick, but enough to give them a slight pout. Her short cut blond hair, that framed her face and descended down over her ears to a few inches above her shoulders, emphasized her cuteness. She had had a few boyfriends since high school. She had slept with two of them. But Randy was the real thing. They had made love about eight hours ago. It was sweet and passionate and loving. And now this man was going to....

She burst into tears. She grabbed the sides of her russet colored parka. It had been unzippered all night since the heat was on in the car, but she had decided to leave it on to hide her body. She pulled the parka tight around her body now and wrapped her arms around herself. "Please don't," she whimpered. "Please."

"You know," he responded, "I could jump over that bed and be on top of you before you could even begin to scream. I'd first break every bone in your face with my fist. Then I'd tie you up and really go to work. And then I'd fuck you anyway and you'd have gone through all that for nothing. So don't be stupid. Take off your clothes and do it now."

His voice was cold and certain. She was sure he would do all those things. The vision of her face all bloody and pulpy came into her head along with all the other things he could do to her. Tears were streaming down her face. She had been scared when she was kidnapped, but now a fierce terror ran right through her, stronger even than that. The urge to vomit came over her again and she fought it off. Her heart was thumping away madly. She could hear her blood rushing in her ears. The man made a move as if to get up from his chair. She sprang to her feet, panicked. "I'll do it! I'll do it!" she screeched.

The man relaxed. "Okay, then do it. And stand over here where I can see you better." He pointed to the foot of the bed, some four feet away from where he sat.

Slowly, cautiously, Carly edged her way over to the spot. She took off her parka and let it drop to the floor. Her skimpy yellow dress showed off her attributes nicely. Her thighs were well toned and her hips were sweet. The dress had a semicircular bodice, just above the rise of her grapefruit sized breasts, with puffy half sleeves that went down to just below her elbows. Her tan, sheer nylons, made her long legs seem graceful and alluring. Her yellow pumps brought her appropriately erect and jutted her breasts into presentation position. She cringed as his eyes flowed over her.

She had to pee. He would beat her if she peed while he was fucking her. She was sure of that. She was so scared she could barely hold it in. She pressed her thighs together. "I have to use the bathroom," she said to him meekly.

He laughed. "Okay! Okay! Go ahead," he said mirthfully.

She went around the bed to the bathroom. The door was open. She flicked on the light. It was like the old man had said. It had been recently redone in a dark blue tile that went up the wall about five feet. The toilet was sparkly new. There was a long tub with a shower curtain, light blue with little green, red and yellow fishes swimming on it. The vanity was painted light blue and the walls above the tile were bright white. There was a dark green oval throw rug on the floor. The old man had put a lot of money in it. That's why he got extra for the place.

She turned to close the door and saw that the man had followed her around the bed. He pushed his hand forward and held the door open. She got the message. She went to the toilet, reached under her frilly yellow skirt and pulled her panties, a white silk thong, down to her ankles. She squatted, closed her eyes and let it go.

"Why me? Why me? Why me?" she kept repeating to herself. The sound of her liquids hitting the water below her echoed through the small room. It soon faded. The man was standing right next to her. She wiped herself and stood, pulling up her panties, and her body bumped into his. She bounced off and he didn't move a millimeter. She went to leave.

"Stay here," he told her. He grabbed her wrist with his left hand. With his right, he drew down the zipper to his pants and fished out his cock. It was thick and springy, like it had begun to fill with blood but had not quite finished. His grip was tight and secure, like a handcuff over her wrist. She closed her eyes while listening to him piss. When the drops ended and she felt him do a little wiggle before restoring himself, she opened her eyes again.

He pulled her out into the bedroom and to her spot. He sat down in the chair and looked at her. "Okay," he said. "Strip."

Carly looked at him forlornly for a second and then, when she saw impatience creep into his face, she reached behind her over her shoulders and undid the clasp at the top of her dress.

She pulled the zipper part way down and then lowered her arms and brought them behind her again. She was keeping her vision to the floor, not wanting to watch him watch her. She got the zipper down to her waist and was about to pull the dress off of her shoulders when the man said, "Slowly."

His voice was like a rapier right through her. He had utter control over her. He could make her do anything he wanted. All because she was afraid of the terrible pain he could cause her. She felt like a coward. She hated herself. She hated him. She did as he said.

Slipping the dress slowly over one shoulder at a time, she let the bodice fall slowly to her hips. Its fall revealed her lacy bra, half cups, worn specially for Randy. For his eyes only. And now this beast was polluting it. She knew that her frilly attire would egg the man on. There was nothing she could do about it now.

She put her thumbs inside the waistband of the dress and slowly shimmied her hips until it slid over her them. Rather than let it fall, and perhaps, in her mind, to slow the revelation of her slim, shiny, white panties, she bent over and lowered it gradually, realizing at the last moment that she was giving him a wondrous display of her breasts. She felt them shift as she leaned over. The bra pushed them together nicely, despite its skimpiness, and she knew that the man was getting a view of the dark tunnel of her cleavage. She pressed her lips together tightly to suppress a whine. She didn't want to give him the benefit of it. She was going to keep her feelings to herself. He could have her body, but not her emotions. She would do what he said, but remove herself from it as much as possible. It would be like fucking a mannequin as far as she was concerned.

When the dress was to her ankles, she stepped out of it, one leg at a time. "Give it to me," the man said gruffly.

She handed it to him, at first without looking, and then when he didn't take it, she looked up. He was grinning. He took it from her hand. "Keep going," he said. "This is great." He tossed the dress aside.

"Twelve years," she thought. "Twelve years without a woman. What passions had built up inside him? What was fucking him going to be like? She was sure it would be brutal and nasty. His hands were as big as bread plates. They would soon be all over her, pawing her, poking her, despoiling her. She tried to put that out of her mind.

She decided that the stockings would be next. She started to kick off her lemon yellow pumps.

"No," he said suddenly, "Leave them on for now. The stockings too. They look nice."

Carly suppressed a sob. If not the stockings or the shoes, there were only two other things left. "Fuck it," she thought, rendering an uncharacteristic profanity. She straightened her back and reached behind her with both hands. She felt her breasts bulge out. She undid the clasp expertly, like she had a thousand times before. She brought her arms back before her, crossed her arms and drew the bra off of her shoulders and then her breasts. Carelessly, she let the bra slip from her right hand into her left and dropped it on the floor.

She didn't hide her breasts. She didn't slump her shoulders. She just looked at the man coldly. "There, you see," she tried to say wordlessly, "that's all you get. Not the inside. Just the outside."

The man smiled. She then hooked her thumbs in the waistband of her panties, drew it out and slowly brought them down over her thighs, then her knees and then to her ankles. She carefully stepped out of them, making sure not to catch her heels and dropped them on top of the bra. There. She was naked. So what.

The man sat there admiring her for a while. "Twelve years," she thought. "Twelve years." She was looking at the wall behind him, avoiding his gaze, but not directing it downwards from fear or shame. Despite herself, when he got up, she flinched.

"Put your hands on your head and spread your legs," the man ordered her. "And close your eyes," he added.

Carly did as she was bid. Her nervousness was coming back. Not being able to see him made things seem different. He had power; he could see. She had none.

She sensed and heard him moving around her. He circled her once and then again, stopping when he was behind her. His hands came from around her sides and took possession of her breasts.

The hands were hot and strong. They felt rough on her breasts' tender skin. But his touch was gentle, like he had cupped two little delicate birds in his hands. The heat of his hands went right through her. He was standing right behind her, his chest pressed into her shoulders, his belt into the small of her back. Carly had been one of the tallest girls in her class, or at least in the upper tenth percentile. But this guy made her feel tiny. Her resolve to remain neutral and detached was ebbing away. The hands could not be ignored as they gently caressed her breasts, squeezing them softly, running their thumbs over her nipples lightly, surrounding her breasts like they were small creatures caught in tender traps. She could feel her heart beating. Her body was beginning to sweat. She could feel her knees trembling. She could feel his stiffened cock against the top of her ass.

Then, one arm went around her waist. The other hand descended her belly, lower and lower, spreading a hot caress. She flinched when she felt it and she cursed herself for it. The hand played momentarily with the sparse, blond hair that bearded her loins. Then it went down lower, drifting lightly over her mons. Two thick fingers traced the outline of her crevasse, on the outside, between her outer labial lips and her thighs. The man was leaning over her and she could feel his hot breath in her ear. The fingers went delicately, up and down, up and down, slowly, several times. It was tantalizing. She wanted to bring her legs together to deny him this touch, but two things stopped her. One was her obvious fear of him and what he might do if she moved without permission. In the bathroom she had gotten a look in the mirror at her right arm and the large, deep purple bruise that had arisen there.

The second was that to move was to confess her responses to his touch. She could feel a warmth arising from her loins. She felt a thick finger probe at the entrance to her womb. It sank into her just a smidgeon and drew a line from her perineum to the apex of her slit. Then it went back down again. She knew that she had gotten wet because the finger slid so smoothly along her crevasse. The finger probed a little deeper, just up to its first knuckle. She felt her outer lips pushed aside by it, actually felt it within her. Her body shuddered and she bit her bottom lip. She kept her eyes clasped tightly shut.

Then, after two or three more traverses, it sank deeper. There was no denying it now. He was inside her. When the finger reached the top of her velvety cavern, it rubbed a bit back and forth across the top, hitting the spot that drove her wild. She issued a little moan and cursed herself again. It wasn't fair what the man was doing to her. He should just get on with it. She didn't want to respond to his caresses, didn't want the pleasure they were bringing. She wanted him to fuck her and get it over with. But that was not the man's plan.

He chuckled when he heard her moan. He twirled the tip of his finger over her clitoris a few times. Carly experienced a rush of pleasurable sensations. She bent her waist and tried to draw her hips back, but the man was stronger and bigger than her and she could not remove her pussy from his reach. He slipped two fingers into her vagina, almost all the way, slid them back and forth in her energized hole until she moaned again. Then he withdrew his hand, chuckling again, and released her.

He stepped away. She kept her eyes closed, her hands on her head. She was woefully self conscious of her nudity, the only nude thing in the room. She heard him moving around and then the sound of him cracking open a bottle. She knew what it was. It was the Jim Beam. She had been waiting for when he started on the booze. The idea of him drunk frightened her. He was callous and cruel sober. What would he be like with a load on?

The sound of crinkling paper struck her ears and then the sound of a pouring liquid. The bottle was put down on the table. He stepped around her and went to the small kitchen sink. She heard the faucet running for a moment or two. Then it stopped. He stepped in front of her.

"Go sit on the bed," he told her.

She opened her eyes. He was standing in front of her, the glass of sour mash in his right hand. She quietly obeyed him, knowing that by going to the bed, she was one step closer to her ravishment. She went to the head of the bed and snuggled up against the headboard as if it offered some protection.

He followed her there and then held out the glass. "Here," he said. "Drink this."

She looked at him unhappily. While she had been standing she had been able to summon her reserves of strength to maintain her dignity and pride, but sitting on the bed, naked, with him towering over her, she lost her aplomb. She scrunched her shoulders and pulled her legs together. She didn't want to drink the alcohol. The messages of lust he had sent her with his hands were bad enough without the effects of liquor. But he knew that. That's why he was doing it.

"The booze is for you," he said. "I don't drink. Never have. It's for suckers. Take the glass and do what I say and things will remain nice and calm and peaceful between us."

Carly cringed at the thought of them being otherwise. She took the glass in her hand and took a sip. She was never a big drinker and she didn't like the taste of hard liquor, even when it was diluted with water. But she knew that she had to do what she was told.

While she sat and held the glass, taking little baby girl sips, he went over to her pocketbook that was still lying on the bed. He picked it up and rummaged through it, emerging with the little tin she used to keep her joints in. Randy had given them to her. She liked to take a toke or two before she went to bed at night. She usually didn't carry the tin in her purse. She had a special drawer for it at home. Randy had run out for once and she had brought it over. She cringed when she saw him pop the lid and remove a sleek, expertly rolled joint.

He put the tin back and tossed her pocketbook onto the floor. Pulling a lighter from his pants pocket, he lit it, took a toke, blowing it out without breathing it in, and then handed it to her. "Smoke it," he told her. He put the ash tray on the bed next to her.

She took the joint from him and put it in her mouth. She took a little puff. The last thing she wanted was to be stoned. She didn't think she could handle what was coming if she was drunk and stoned. He saw her emit a small puff of smoke.

"I'll give you a choice, cunt," he told her, agitated now. "You can smoke that joint right or I'll shove it up your ass! And that would be just for starters! Got it?"

Carly whined but nodded her head. She took a deep toke of the joint into her lungs and held it there for about ten seconds. The she let it all out. She got a rush right away. Randy did always have good weed. This was the best he had had in a while. The room seemed to grow larger and smaller all at the same time.

The man left her to sip at her drink and smoke the joint. He sat on a chair in front of the bed and began to untie his boots. She tried not to watch him, but her eyes just seemed to drift to him naturally. She took another sip of liquor and another toke of the joint. "Maybe it would be better if I was wacked out of my mind," she thought. "Maybe I won't remember it as well then. It'll be just like some kind of horrible dream that I can put behind me."

His boots were off and he pulled off his socks. White ones. He reached to his waist and pulled his undershirt up over his head. There were more tattoos on his muscular chest. His chest was not as hairy as she expected, almost hairless, in fact. He tossed the t-shirt to the side and stood up. He released his belt and his fly and drew his pants down revealing a sparkling white pair of boxer shorts. His cock and balls formed a lump in the appropriate place. Carly looked away.

He got up and moved towards her. She felt a weakness in her belly. When he was a foot away from her, towering way up high, he told her to take another toke of the joint. When she finished, he took it away. "I don't want you too wigged out," he said. "Finish the drink."

He tossed the joint into the ash tray, put it on the table and then walked to the standing lamp next to the bed on the other side. He turned it on. It cast a soft light on the bed. While he was there, he drew down the shade on the small window on that side. He walked over to the door. There was a brass chain lock on the door and he slid the end into the slot. He turned out the overhead light. The room went from a garish brightness to a soft, mellow tone. The hollow feeling in Carly's belly got worse as she knew the moment of truth was coming. He stood next to her. She had finished about half of the booze. Her head was getting woozy. "Drink it all down," he told her. "All at once. Enough fucking around."

Suppressing a sob, Carly tossed the booze back. She gulped it down. He took the glass from her. "Pull down the covers, take off your shoes and get up on the bed," he told her.

A numb feeling passed through her. Her hands were shaking. She pulled the covers down to the foot of the bed. She lifted the comforter at the end and tucked them under it. Then she slipped off her slender, yellow pumps, happy to have them off after such a long while, and got on the bed. The mattress was firm but resilient. The old man had not cheaped out on it. She scurried to the other side, nearer to the bathroom. She couldn't tell what the man was doing. He had his back to her and was holding something. A center of light fell on the bed, but the rest of the room was still dark. She guessed that it was close to 6 in the morning and that the sun would be coming up soon. She had been his prisoner for 6 hours. Now he was going to fuck her. She sat with her back against the headboard, drew up her knees, put her hands over her face and softly cried.

She felt the bed depress when he got on it. He lay down next to her and put his hand on her ankle. "Scrunch down, and move to the middle," he told her while he pulled on it. Carly knew that she would only be delaying the inevitable by resisting. The light from the lamp was shining directly on where they would be fucking. Her body felt cold with fear. She shuffled her body down towards the foot of the bed. Her knee brushed up against him and she looked at him. He was naked. His cock, thick and long, surrounded by a thicket of black, curly hair, was rampant. "Oh, god!" she thought.

He was leaning on his side. There was something in his hand. She was flat on her back. She felt puny next to him.

"Put your hands in front of you," he told her. She looked at him. "Do it!" he insisted. Afraid of him striking her, him being so close, she obeyed fretfully. What was he going to do?

Then she saw the rope.

"Oh, please don't tie me," she whined plaintively. "Please." A deep chill went through her. "I'll do whatever you say. Please!"

"Shut the fuck up!" he told her gruffly. Her body began to tremble and fear invaded her whole being. "Why is he tying me up?" she thought dismally. "What's he going to do?"

He tied one end of the rope to her left wrist and pulled it tight. Then he brought her hands together, wrist to wrist and circled the two of them twice. He ran the rope between them twice and then around and then between them once again and tied it off. They were forced tightly together. The fingers of her right and left hands were touching.

Pulling her hands above her head, he threaded the rope through one of the gaps in the headboard, right in the center of the bed. There were two rows of decorative cutouts, one low, about four or five inches from the bottom of the headboard, and one row about another foot or so towards the top. He circled the rope around the wood between two cutouts on the bottom and then pulled the free end up to the higher cutout. He tied the end off there, once, twice, three times, pulling it tighter than Carly ever could strain to get it apart.

Even if she could reach it, that is. Since her hands were tied to the lower level of cutouts, she wouldn't be able to reach the higher. If she got up on her knees, and turned around, she might be able to use her teeth to untie the top knot, but it would take a long time and she was sure he wouldn't leave her alone for that long. She was effectively tied in place. He lowered himself next to her and brought his body close. His cock jutted up against her right thigh. She bit her lip and moaned unhappily.

He was leaning on his elbow. His wild, black hair was highlighted by the light that shown down on it. His face had a fierce intentness. His tattoos made him seem demonic, his beard, cruel. She closed her eyes. She could feel his body's heat, smell his sweat. Her legs were jammed together. The room was spinning.

She felt his hand, his big, meaty, right hand, slide slowly over her knees, then her thighs and then her belly. It took hold of a breast and squeezed it gently. He flicked his thumb over her nipple, which had turned stiff from fear, or maybe passion, since the feeling he had arisen in her before was coming alive again. He moved his hand to her other breast, circled it, caressed it, squeezed it. Her breasts were not small by any means. They were plump and firm and resisted gravity. But they seemed small compared to the hugeness of his hands.

His hand ran down her belly again and over her compressed thighs and back up again. Its heat communicated right through her stockings, which she still wore, a refined decoration, meant not for him, but for another whose arms she had been in only hours before. But now they were for him. She could see in her mind's eye her long and slender legs, encased in shiny, smooth, sheer, mauve. At the tops, there were black lacy decorations sewn into it. Her thighs were pale and she knew that the contrast between the dark, sheik, luxurious encasings below, and her tender, soft, inviting white thighs was tantalizing. That was why she wore them. But not for him! Not for him!

Wherever it went, his hand spread his heat and his power. She felt her pussy begin to hum and she gritted her teeth, squelched her eyes closed to try and stop it, but the hand kept moving up and down her body, caressing her breasts, teasing her belly and thighs, even down her shins and back again. He pulled and pinched her nipples, gently at first, and then harder and harder until she moaned from the pain. He spread his hand over her neck and up over her face, covering it, while he nestled up against her and kissed her throat. His lips were hot and his tongue scoured over her vibrating flesh. He placed his hand on the side of her face and turned her head towards him. "Open your mouth," he said softly.

A flash of sickness ran through her as she thought of his tongue in her mouth, but she obeyed. She had no choice. She tried not to imagine the things he would do to her if she resisted. He leaned his face closer to hers, his huge hand holding her head still and he brought their lips together. She tasted his hot breath, sour and manly, the bristles of his beard brushing up against her cheek. His lips covered hers and his tongue, huge, insistent, fiercely hot, slipped slowly into her mouth.

"Ohhhhhhhhhhh," she moaned in spite of herself. A wave of pleasure went through her. The booze and the weed had broken down the mental block she had tried to impose against pleasure. He kissed her deeply, his tongue tasting every corner of her mouth, dancing with her own, inflaming her. She felt her left knee rise of its own accord. Her hands twisted in their bonds. She breathed deep and tried futilely to move her head away, to snatch back the last vestige of resistance she had, but he held her face still with his mighty paw.

Then, she gave in. She kissed him back. Sensing the end of her will to resist, his hand fluttered down over her breasts and belly again. She let her leg drop and the hand washed over her thighs. It came back again and seized her breasts, making her moan. And then slowly, slowly, slowly, it crossed her belly and approached the apex of her thighs. He broke their kiss. "Spread your legs," he told her.

His voice broke the spell his tongue had worked on her. She remembered where she was, what he was doing to her, what he might do later when she was of no more use to him. His coarseness, the two rock solid blows he had given her, his inner cruelty, all came back to her. She had kissed him! His tongue had been in her mouth! Now he was going to touch her there, just like he had done before. He was going to stoke her fires, make her moan, drive her lusts. She wanted to resist, tried to resist, but the hand that insinuated itself between her thighs easily moved them apart, as if they were in cahoots with him, had rebelled against her, and wanted only the pleasure that his ministrations would bring.

She felt his hand slip over her love lips and mesh itself in her sparse, blond moss. It slipped back again and a finger traced a line between her outer labia. It did it again. And then again. And then again. She moaned and her rebellious thighs spread wider still.

He brought his hand up and captured her face, turning it again towards him, pressing his lips against hers and begging entry with his tongue. Her mouth opened. His tongue entered and she moaned. The hand slipped down over her torso again, stopping momentarily to caress and squeeze her now rock hard breasts, and then descended below. When his finger found the button at the apex of her vulva, when it spread her moisture over it and caressed it, her back arched and she groaned.

Having her mouth and pussy excited both at the same time was too much for her. It overwhelmed her, flung her into another universe. Her mind was whirling, the pot and booze had made her body seem both soft and welcoming and excited beyond redemption all at the same time.

His fingers probed deeply within her and began a slow, steady rhythm, sliding back and forth in her energized crevasse while his thumb pressed down on her clit, massaging it, flicking it softly, circling it and rubbing it. It went on for several minutes, making her madder and madder with lust. She felt her crisis coming. Her mind panicked. "No! No! No!" she thought frantically. But nothing could stop it. Her pussy erupted into a paroxysm of pleasure. It throbbed and pulsed and spasmed and clenched and she groaned and moaned into her captor's mouth. Her heels dug into the bed and her hands twisted and writhed up above her. "Oh god! Oh, god! Oh, god!" she called out in her mind.

As her pussy's spasms slowed, the hand abandoned its task again, spreading its warmth over her belly and breasts once more. His tongue remained in her mouth, but became less insistent. She was lost in a fog of swirling feelings all over her body.

Then, she felt the man's thigh cross hers. It was hot and heavy. It spread her other leg further apart and she felt the other one cross. His hips were between her knees. "He's going to fuck me!' she thought, panicked. "He's going to fuck me! Oh, god, please don't let him do it! Please!"

He broke their kiss. His hand went over her body again, twisting and turning her breasts, harder now than before, with authority and dominance. They were his, not hers. All of her was his. Her body was his. Her pussy was his. His whole demeanor, his strength, his callousness and lust proclaimed it.

It was stupid, she knew. She was ashamed at her baseness later, the next day, when she thought about it. But some part of her thought it possible, that if she just asked him, begged him, pleaded with him, he wouldn't do it. He would abandon his intent, respect her declination. Grant her mercy.

"Please don't do this," she whined desperately. "Pllleeeeeeeease! Plllllleeeeeeeeeeease! Don't fuck me! Pleeeeeeeeease! I don't want to! I don't want to, pleee-eeeeease! Pleeeeeeeeease!"

His mighty hand grabbed her cheeks and clasped them hard. She squealed from the pain. He made her look at him. "Shut the fuck up!" he hissed. "If you talk out of turn one more time, I'll make you hurt like you never hurt before! I'm going to fuck you, cunt, and you're going to open up and your going to make me feel good or you'll be real sorry. Got that?"

Carly whined a terrorized response. Her body was trembling. His thighs pressed hers wider. "Lift your knees," he told her. She lifted them. He was nestled on top of her. His hand went down to his crotch. She felt the head of his cock slip along her labial lips. It sent a wave of electricity through her. She was crying silently, but her mind was focused all so intently on the spot of contact between their loins. "That was his cock," she thought. "His cock. Oh, god! Oh, god!"

Then, to her surprise, he didn't enter her. Instead, she felt the head of his manhood slide slowly up and down her crevasse, dipping ever so slightly in, like he was teasing her. Her rebellious pussy yearned to be filled. She wanted to bring her legs together, but he was between them. She spread them, instead, as widely as she could to forestall the contact between her sensitive, burning inner thighs and his hips. He was balancing himself on his other hand and the only part of him that was touching her was his cock. The cock kept sliding up and down. She wanted it to go away. She wanted it to enter her. She wanted him to fuck her. No! She didn't want that! She wanted him to melt away into a fog as if he had never been here, as if she were in her own bed, in her own apartment and all this had been some horrible dream. But the ropes on her wrists were not a dream. Her aching pussy was not a dream. His leering face, his demonic eyes, his wild hair, his broad chest, his meaty hands, hands that had already claimed her as his, they were not a dream.

He leaned forward. He placed his mouth on hers. His chest lay against her breasts, forcing them down with his weight. His tongue entered her mouth. All her senses concentrated on it as its heat spread within her, as her own tongue greeted it with glee. He kissed her hard, for a long, long time.

And then she felt it. His cock was moving forward. Slowly, slowly, slowly, it edged its way inside her. Her tongue was flitting wildly with his, but her pussy was absolutely still, waiting to be impaled. His cock was thick. She could feel it filling her. It was creating a buzzing sensation all over her body. Her pussy screamed its welcome, sending trilling vibrations down her spasming legs.   It went on and on and on. She didn't think she could tolerate it for one more second. And then it stopped. His hips were pressed against hers. Their bellies matched. He was sunk deep within her. He was fucking her! He was fucking her! "Oh, god! Oh, god! Oh, god, please no!" her mind screamed.

When he began his movements, her prayers evaporated, subsumed by the overwhelming sensation of his cock scouring her womb. He started slow, slipping his cock back and forth leisurely, smoothly. Carly felt about to burst. How he could maintain such self control was beyond her. She wanted him to go faster. Yearned for him to go faster. She couldn't stand teetering on the precipice like this. It was agony.

Then their mouths separated. He raised his head. His hands came on either side of her face, holding her head still. His motions were increasing. She could barely breathe. "He's going to come inside me!" she thought suddenly, panicked. She didn't want that! She didn't want that! "Oh, please stop! Please stop!" she thought madly. She closed her eyes again to try and blot out what was happening. She didn't want to see his face, wanted to deny him. But his thoughts were different. He pressed his thumbs on her eyelids and lifted them. Her eyes came open wide. His eyes peered into them, gleeful, taunting, powerful, cruel. His motions were going faster and faster. She could feel the strength of his thrusts. Her body was shuddering at each impact. Her pussy was screaming with need. "Oh, god! Oh, god! Oh, god!" she thought. She moaned, groaned, cried out, "Ohhhhh! Ohhhhhhhh! Ohhhhhhh!" as her pussy began a series of fierce contortions. "Ohhhhhh! Ohhhhhhh! Ohhhhhhh!" she screamed again.

And then he groaned too. His eyes rolled back. His face became tense. His body contracted. He was thrusting wildly into her. "Arrrrrrrrrgh!" he cried. Arrrrrgh! Arrrrrrrrgh! Arrrrrrrrgh! Arrrrrrrrrgh!"

She came again, her hands writhing, her legs wound around his thighs. He was emptying himself inside her. Her mind winced with unhappiness as her pussy celebrated its achievement. "Ohhhhhhhhh! Ohhhhh-hhhhh!" she cried again.

His thrusts slowed. His body relaxed. His face turned placid. He was breathing heavy, but the rest of him was at rest. He continued to slip himself back and forth. Her pussy glowed and she shuddered each time an echo of her orgasms made her pussy clench.

Carly's mind slipped away somewhere. She couldn't tell where it was, but it was foggy and distant. The still hardened cock was still within her, running back and forth desultorily. He was leaning on his elbows, his weight off of her. His eyes were closed. Her legs lost their tension and she let her knees slide down. It was over. It had happened. A tinge first, then a smidgeon, then, suddenly, a wave of remorse washed through her. He had made her scream out in pleasure. He had used her like a whore and she had opened her legs like one. She began to cry again. She turned her head and closed her eyes. But at least it was over. It was over.

But was it over? He was still hard. He was still inside her. He was still moving, now with a little more energy. "Don't, please," she thought miserably. "Don't." The cock kept plunging back and forth, delivering a steady, thrilling, unignorable sensation to the walls of her crevasse that kept building and building and building. Her pussy was warming again. Her thighs trembled. She wanted with all her mind and heart and will to take hold of the relentless plow and stop it, hold it still, stop it from moving, snuff out the delirious sensations her cleft was sending her. But she had no power over it. Her hands were vestigial. She imagined holding it between her hands, clenching it tightly, gripping it as hard as her feminine muscles would allow, but even in her mind she could not stop it. Only he had the power. Only he could stop it. And he would not.

His thrusts were coming harder now. Her pussy was eager once again. She bit her lip, wanting to beg him to stop, to plead with him to stop. But she was terrified of him. He said he would hurt her and she believed him. If only she had at least her hands to defend herself. There was no escape. It kept going, going, going and going!

Suddenly he stopped. He slipped his cock from within her and knelt back. "Turn over and get on your knees," he told her, his passion like the rough edge of a broken glass.

"Oh, god, no," she whined inside.

"Get up!" he thundered.

He reared his hand back and gave her a vicious slap across her breasts. She screeched. He did it again. "Get up!" he yelled.

Sobbing madly, Carly rolled to her belly and got to her knees. She sensed his hand rearing back again and then felt a vicious fire across her buttock. And then another and then another. She screamed and sobbed.

"When I tell you to get on your knees, you'll get on your knees!" he spat out at her harshly. He struck her brutally two more times. She hung her head and sobbed. She felt him position himself behind her. His hands reached in and spread her thighs. He angled her buttocks upwards. She felt his cock probing at her slit. It found it, and then was in.

She cried and cried while he fucked her. His thrusts were hard and fast. Her body shook again and again. Her face was down between her outstretched arms. He had left enough slack on the rope that bound her to the bed so that she had been able to turn over without twisting them. He had planned ahead, like always. Her breasts were pressed against her thighs. The fierce, foul invader kept going on and on. And her pussy, her betrayer, her very own Iago, reveled in it.

He was so big. His body seemed to surround her. It was like a monster had taken possession of her. In this position, the man's thick cock abraded her clitoris with each stroke. She gritted her teeth trying to deny her growing lust, but it was of no use. The cock went on and on. His hot hands were on her hips, holding her body in place, using it as a pivot so that he could thrust himself unmercifully against her buttocks. She cried and cried even as her passions grew. When her explosion came she buried her face in the mattress and screamed. She could feel her pussy clenching the rabid tool that was flaying her again and again. The man groaned. He yelled. He made one! two! three! four! five! mighty thrusts against her, and then he was done.

He lay against her for a while, while he recovered his breath. She was too worn out to cry. What was the use? Some fiendish devil had ordained this awful fate for her and there was no way to avoid it. She felt his softened tool slip from her vagina. "At last," she thought. "At last."

He rose from the bed. He leaned over and untied her hands from the headboard. "If you've got to pee, do it now," he told her. She struggled up from the bed, her hands still bound before her, the rope that had tied her to the bed trailing from her wrists. Following him into the bathroom, she turned her head so that she would not have to look as his cock performed. Then it was her turn. She ignored his looming presence and let her water flow. He had bought some toothbrushes and toothpaste and he made her brush her teeth, which was difficult with her hands tied, but she managed it. Carly figured that it was not out of concern for her, but because he liked putting his tongue in there and didn't want her to have trench mouth.

He went back to her purse and got her cold cream and made her take her makeup off. She tried not to look at herself in the mirror too much, but she could not avoid it. There she was, standing naked, her breasts out and shimmering as she moved. Her nipples seemed like two mournful eyes peering back at her, condemning her for her bout of passion. "Slut!" they said. "Harlot! Jezebel! Weakling!" He was standing next to her, watching her ritual, an ominous presence. When she looked up, she caught his eyes, dark, brooding, merciless eyes. She looked away.

He let her drink some water and then made her stand in the middle of the room with her hands on her head while he had a smoke, sitting in the chair and scouring her with his eyes. She felt his come leaking down her thigh. When he finished, he told her to get on the bed.

To her relief, he untied her hands. But when he told her to lie on her belly, she grew concerned. He told her to put her hands behind her back and he tied them off there. Her heart sank. He went away for a moment and returned with another length of rope. After removing her stockings, he crossed her ankles and tied them off too. Then he stepped away once again and returned with the rubber ball and the duct tape.

"Open your mouth," he told her

She grimaced, now understanding what the ball was for. She wanted to beg him not to do it, but she opened her mouth without saying a word. He forced the ball in her mouth. It made her teeth separate. He tore off a strip of duct tape and covered her mouth.

"Get the message?" he asked her. She tearfully turned her head away. She got the message. No more talking.

He turned off the standing lamp. Hints of the dawn were seeping in past the curtains. He got in bed next to her, to her right, and pulled up the covers. Within a minute, she heard his heavy breathing. He was asleep.

CHAPTER TWO

His real name was John. John Jackson. But everybody called him Blackjack, or just plain Jack. He awoke suddenly, alert and prepared for the worst, just like he had awakened every morning for the last 12 years. The room was flooded with light. It took him a second to realize where he was, but then it all came back to him in a rush.

Yesterday, about 3 p.m., he was being driven down Route 4 on his way to the State Penitentiary in Wolverton. They were coming back from a medical appointment at the cancer specialist hospital in Delberg. He had bribed one of the technicians in the medical ward in the prison to switch his x-rays with one of the con's who was dying of lung cancer. He had made the trip up in the back seat of an unmarked Prison Service car. While at the hospital, while no one was looking, he had snatched a long, thick, surgical knife off a medical tray. In prison, you got nothing if you were not surreptitious. Blackjack had developed it into an art. It was all about the swiftness of his hands and his cool demeanor.

On the way back, he had told the guards that he had to piss. They stopped at a service station. One of the guards followed him into the small bathroom. There was a chain between his ankles and around his waist. Since the guard didn't want to hold his prick while he pissed, he released one hand from the manacles around his waist. When Jack had done shaking his cock, he turned and plunged the knife right into the guard's heart. He coughed, his eyes rolled back and he dropped to the floor.

It took only a few seconds for Jack to get the key to his cuffs and ankle chain from the guard's pocket. He unlocked them, but left them on. Then he opened the door to the bathroom and stepped out a few feet.

"Corporal Davis!" he yelled. "Corporal Davis! I think something has happened to Officer Maynard. I think he's had a heart attack!"

From what Corporal Davis could see, Jack still had his manacles on. He had been standing by the car waiting for the two of them to come out. He ran to the bathroom. It was tough for him to get in with the other guard lying on the floor. Jack went in first. Corporal Davis followed him. He had just leaned over to see what was the matter with Maynard when Jack reached around and slit his throat. He dropped to the floor.

Jack reached into his pocket and got the keys to the car. He thought of taking their guns, but he didn't want to spend time taking off their belts. He didn't even rifle through their pockets for cash. He tossed off the manacles and ran to the car. He got in the driver's side, revved up the engine and took off.

He figured it would be maybe a half hour at best until someone went into the bathroom and found the bodies. Maybe longer if he was lucky, but that was all he could count on. He drove as fast as he could, but careful to stay within the speed limit. They had gotten off the Interstate. He got back on it for twenty miles or so and then got back off. The Interstate was too easy to monitor. It would be the first place they would look for him. He rode along a county road for about 30 miles. He figured that by now word would have gotten back to the prison of his escape.

All hell would brake loose. Soon every cop in the state would be looking for a black, late model Ford Eclipse with state government plates. He needed to ditch it.

It was about 5 when he saw a dirt road on his right that looked just right. He rode down it. It led to on old lumberjack road. He followed the dirt pathway for a couple of miles and then pulled into a stand of Evergreens so that the car couldn't be seen from the air. He got out and took stock. It was too bad it was late January because all the leaves were gone. It was cold too, and would get colder at night. He needed to get somewhere where he could hijack a car. He would need to either kill or kidnap the owner so that the car wouldn't be reported stolen for at least 12 hours. He could be a few hundred miles away by then.

Jack had grown up in the woods. He had no fear of any man or beast. Outside the car, he took a moment to relish his first moment of freedom for 12 years. He was doing a life bid. In this state, life meant life. Sometimes they released on humanitarian grounds some 80 year old lifer who had a couple of months to live. This way he would be buried on the dime of some other state agency. He and his local chapter of the Rouges Motorcycle Club had all been indicted and convicted on a state racketeering beef. They had been manufacturing and distributing crystal meth, ran a nice, profitable prostitution ring, trafficked in stolen cars, extortion, loansharking and whatever else made money. As president of the chapter, Jack got to break in the new girls, willing or unwilling, who they were putting out on the game or were assigning out to chapter members to use as their slaves. Girls that were too much trouble they sold to a Salvadorian gang who marketed them to inner city pimps or to Mexico and beyond.

Maintaining a criminal empire like that required fierce discipline and the ability to strike fear into anyone they dealt with. So of course there had to be a few bodies along the way. Jack liked to keep the killings to a minimum since they attracted too much law enforcement attention. But, of course, motorcycle outlaws were not easy to control. It was kind of like herding cats.

One of the members, Skeeter Mascola, had killed a citizen in broad daylight in front of about 30 witnesses. Now, the code said that he had to take his medicine. He would be taken care of on the inside. Drugs were readily available, as was sex, although the sex was with punk kids doing their first bids for burglary or low level drug distribution. But Skeeter, who was always a bit of a weasel, decided to flip rather than spend the rest of his days marking time. He gave the state attorney general everything. They went to trial and were all convicted, all 20 of them. It made headlines all over the country.

Skeeter didn't live long. A guy like that didn't prosper in the witness protection program. He was running a small heroin ring out on the peninsula when one of the boys from another chapter spotted him. He and his skaggy girlfriend were buried out in the woods where nobody would ever find them.

That was 12 years ago. And now he was out. He knew that the odds were against him, that eventually he would be caught. But he was determined that that day would be the last that he ever woke up in a jail cell. He knew that all he had to do was hook up with a Rouges chapter in another city and they would set him up with whatever he wanted, a new i.d., maybe even some plastic surgery. He didn't want to hook up with any chapters too close to his home state since they were both too small and would be carefully watched. If he could get to the West Coast or maybe Texas or New Mexico, he would be all right. But first he had to get some wheels that every cop in the state wasn't looking for.

He headed out right into the woods, moving fast. He stayed close to the trees, even though there was no real cover. It was just that if he heard a plane or a coptor he could press himself against a tree and hope not to be seen. He loped along a stream he found for a few miles, it being in a depression where he could fall to the ground easily and hide. He was careful when he came upon any hills, looking up at the sky carefully and keeping a low profile when he crossed them.

He had had lunch at the hospital, a tray of hospital food: a Salisbury steak, some green beans and half a canned peach. But that was hours ago. Corporal Davis had had a lunch bag, but he had eaten most of it except for an apple. Jack ate it after he had been moving for two hours. He knew that he would have to eat if he wanted to keep up his strength, but he also knew that the time at which it would become a real problem was a long way off.

He had been training for years for this escape. He worked out with weights, did exercises to strengthen his legs, spent several days, every couple of months, when he would eat only bread and water. He stayed away from the drugs, although he had been tempted many times. With a life sentence, an interminable string of boring, repetitive days awaited him. It was tempting to be able to take your mind somewhere else and forget where you were. But that was how guys got in trouble. You had to wake up sometime. And when you did, your were still right where you started out. Guys like that got careless and once in a while, one would be found with his throat slit in some remote corner of the prison factory or in a corner of the yard where the screws couldn't see what happened. Or they would just fade away and die.

He was determined not to die in prison. So he kept himself healthy and fit. He had an elevated status in the prison because of his gang connections, he had been the president of a very profitable chapter for about 10 years, and he got the occasional luxury when he wanted it. He got his pick of the punks. The guards treated him okay too because they knew that he kept order and dealt out justice to the other cons judiciously and discretely, usually.

He traveled for hours. He passed an occasional house here or there and was tempted to go in and take what he needed, but home invasion was always risky. You could end up on the wrong side of a .30 shotgun or somebody could get away or make a desperate phone call to the cops. Even if it were successful, somebody might discover the results of his mayhem, he would have to kill everybody in the house, and then they would really be after him, not simply as an escaped con, but as a mass murderer. No, it was best that he be patient and wait for the right opportunity. So far he was ahead of the game and he felt confident that the cops wouldn't find the unmarked Prison Service cars for a few days at least.

He came upon the gas station at a little after 10 that night. It was still a little busy and so he knew that he would have to wait to make his move. The fact of his escape would have been all over the news already. But he could have gone off in a dozen different directions and so he still had the upper hand. Besides, they were still probably looking for the black Eclipse.

When he saw the girl pull up, his heart had lifted. She was alone; she had a rather unremarkable car. The traffic had died down at the station and nobody else had pulled in for a good ten minutes or so. It didn't hurt that she was good looking. She was wearing a rather bulky parka, but it didn't cover her long, pretty legs or her short, appealing blond hair. He had snuck up to the car while she was pumping gas. The passenger door was unlocked. "Stupid cunt," he thought.

Once she got in, it was all over.

Lying there in the motel room bed, he thanked the fates for his good fortune. He awoke this morning a free man. He had gotten laid last night. With a woman. An attractive, hot, obedient woman. And he would get laid today too.

He had restrained himself during their drive last night. Part of him wanted to have her pull up some dark roadway where he would have piled her into the back seat and fucked the shit out of her. But it was more important to make tracks. He had learned a lot of discipline in the pen. It was enough to know that when they finally stopped for the night, she would shortly thereafter be naked, in his bed, and with her legs spread.

And oh, yeah, to be buried in a cunt for the first time in 12 years was heaven. To be able put your tongue in a mouth and not feel whiskers, that was heaven. He hadn't worried too much about whether she would be passionate. He had a lot of experience in these matters and had found that once you lit their candle, most women would be off to the races by the time you stuck your cock in them. That's what his little playtime had been about, when he had her stand naked and he had caressed her until she moaned with lust. That's what the booze and weed had been about. And it had worked like a charm. Yeah, he had to slap her around a little bit to get her to cooperate, but that was par for the course. There had been girls he had had to do a lot worse to. This cunt was getting off easy, even though she probably didn't think so.

She was still asleep. He had worried a little about whether the ropes would hold until the morning, but then he realized that she was so tired she would fall off to sleep long before she would be able to work herself free. Eventually, any knot will give way if you struggled long enough. But all his experience in the woods, and later breaking in whores, had refined his knot tying abilities and his were among the best.

She had her face turned towards him. The silver duct tape covered her mouth down to her chin. He had put on three strips overlaying each other so the whole mouth was covered. All three would have to be worked loose before she could open her mouth. And then she would have to try and get the rubber ball out. When he had seen the display at the convenience store last night he had known that it was just the right size for his purposes.

The rest of her face looked peaceful, as if she didn't have a concern in the world.

He slipped out of bed and stretched. It was the first time he had awoken in a room bigger than 12 by 10 in twelve years. After he had taken a piss, he decided to make coffee. There was a battery operated clock on the wall above the stove and it said that it was a little after 11 o'clock. 5 hours sleep was good enough for him. He didn't know how much the cunt needed so he would let her sleep as long as possible. She would be driving all night. He preferred to have her drive since she actually had a license and the registration was in her name. There was always the possibility that if they got stopped by the cops they would not know that he had kidnapped her yet and would let them go. If not, he was on the other side of the car and would have the chance to slip out and book or quickly come around and take care of the cop.

He quietly pulled down the percolator from the cabinet. He filled it at the small sink next to the stove and then filled the basket with coffee. "Ahhhhhh," he thought. The smell of fresh coffee was wonderful. There were so many everyday things that he had not experienced in more than a decade he could not even begin to count them. One thing for sure was that he would never take any of them for granted again.

He put the coffee on the stove and then recovered his skivvies. Prison issue. They always bleached the hell out of them. He put them on and began his exercise routine. Squats, pushups, leg thrusts, leg raises, sit ups, more pushups, more squats, more sit ups. It was a routine he had perfected many years ago. He did them every morning. They only way to deal with real time in prison, and real time was anything over a couple of years, was to have routines that brought you little bits of pleasure. And working out he always felt energized and ready for the day.

When he was done, he noticed that the girl was awake. He didn't feel like dealing with her and so he left her where she was. She looked at him forlornly. She probably had to pee, but she could wait.

The coffee had been brewing for fifteen minutes or so. The smell was terrific. He took it off the burner and let it settle for a minute and then poured himself a cup in a mug that advertised the State Fair of 1987. He had been just earning his bones in 1987, a kid. He had come up hard, fought all comers. He had been smart, made money for his partners in crime, and lived as free a life as any man could ask for. He answered to no man, took what he wanted, did whatever he wanted. That was the way to live life, not as some wage slave. If it meant dying young or eventual prison, that's just the way it went. It was part of the deal. But while you lived, you really lived.

He took his coffee to the table and set it down. He went over to the bed and pulled the covers up off of the girl. Then he sat down and drank it, smoking his first cigarette of the day, enjoying the view of the naked, bound and gagged toy he had captured. Her helplessness made his cock twitch. Her hands were flopped behind her like a little tail jutting from the base of her back. He liked the fire engine red nails. It was if she had gotten all dolled up just for him. And the toenails, that was a nice touch. Only a girl who was going to take down her panties did her toenails in the wintertime. He wondered if she had been fucking earlier the night before. The condoms and lube in her purse said yes. That made him laugh. He doubted that her boyfriend made her scream and yell like he did.

He recalled the picture of the boy in her wallet. He was just the kind of straight arrow motherfucker he despised. They talked a big game about law and order when they were around each other, but when alone, all you had to do was slap them around a little bit and they would be cowering like mice. To think that a guy like that got to regularly fuck a good looking piece of tail like her. What was her name? He had read it on her license, but he couldn't remember it. It was Carol or something like that. Who cared? As long as she had a hot pussy, and she had a hot one all right, she didn't need a name.

Before he had been picked up on the racketeering warrant, he had had a few hundred pussies. There had been a few he had kept around for a while, ones that were especially pretty or saucy, or who gave particularly good head. But most of them were throw aways. And even the good ones he got rid of after a while, passing them down to lower echeloned members of the club or trading them off to another chapter. There was no way he was ever going to lose his head over a piece of tail. And the best way to keep from getting hooked was to treat them like shit. The worse, the better. It kept them in there place and made them retain their identity as impersonal objects. That and making sure that their status never rose above mere property.

There was an iron clad rule. Once a bitch had been claimed by one of the members of the club, she was claimed for life. She had no say in it, whether she came voluntarily or not. And when you got tired of them, you passed them on or put them on the street to earn.

The girl let out a little whimper. Her eyes were looking at him hopefully. Her hands twisted in their bonds and her legs were pressed together. He recalled with relish his bout with her last night. Twelve years was a long time to go without pussy. Fucking a guy just wasn't the same thing, no matter how young and sweet looking he was. Not to say that it wasn't a pleasure. Once a sweet young punk became his property in the jail, he could do anything he wanted with him. Usually, he put him out earning. And if the kid was coming up for parole, well, there were ways to take care of that too. Some contraband found in his possession, talking back to a guard, a staged fight in the cafeteria. And for the special ones, for a price, the guards would bring him up on new charges, like assaulting an officer. He would get resentenced to a whole new bid and he would be around for a couple more years.

But fucking a cunt was different, so much better that it wasn't even worth talking about it. If it all ended this very moment, he thought, it would have been worth it just to have lived in that little girl's pussy for a while.

He finished his coffee. His cigarette lay stamped out in the ashtray. He decided to give the girl some relief. He didn't want to have to deal with a wet bed. And then he would have to fuck her up for doing something dirty. He preferred not to mark her all up if he didn't have to. Not yet, at least.

He rose from his chair and stepped to the bed. He untied her ankles and then pulled her up to her feet. He led her into the bathroom and put her on the toilet. She looked at him mournfully, her mouth still covered by the silver tape, her arms bound behind her. He just waited. She peed. He stood her up, made her spread her legs and wiped her. The last thing he wanted was a smelly pussy.

He led her back into the room and brought her over to the table. He sat her down in a chair. She brought her legs together and hunched her shoulders like she was trying to hide herself from him.

"Sit up straight," he told her. "And spread your legs. Don't ever try and hide your pussy from me again. Got it?"

The girl's eyes got watery, but she obeyed. She sat back in the chair as far as she could go with her arms behind her and spread her legs.

"Wider," he told her curtly. She spread them so that her knees were on the outsides of the chair. That was better.

He decided he was hungry. He rummaged through one of the bags from the store and brought out a can of stew. It had a pop lid and he broke it open. He went to the cabinet and got a soup spoon and returned. When he was sitting again, he spooned out a bit and put it in his mouth. It might be lukewarm and have only come from a can, but it sure beat prison food.

He ate from the can slowly, savoring every bite. He kept his eyes on the girl, admiring her tits and the rest of her. What a stroke of luck she had been. He would have settled for any old cunt. He had decided in advance that he would kidnap a woman if possible both because a woman would be easier to deal with and because he could fuck her. He would have taken Two Ton Tessie if she had been the only choice. To get prime beef on the hoof was way beyond his expectations. But here she was. And they had just started to have fun.

He scraped up every last bit of the stew and licked the spoon. It had really hit the spot. He tossed the can in the garbage and put the spoon in the sink. Then he poured himself another cup of coffee. He took it black. He had bought the coffee last night on the odd chance he would get the opportunity to make some.   He was glad he did. It was something he had been dreaming about for years.

He went back to his chair. The girl was watching very move he made. He took a sip and put the cup down on the table. He looked at the girl. She had a fine set of tits. Tits were another thing your didn't get in the joint. Hers were just about the perfect size. It would take years before they started to sag, if ever. Right now they were perfectly ripe. They hung nicely and curved just a little up at the ends. And she had nice fat nipples and wide, smooth areolas.

He reached down and to take hold of her nipples. She reared back a little, as much as she could, when she saw his hands coming, but there was nowhere to go. He grabbed them between his thumbs and forefingers and pulled her tits just a little bit out from her body. He gave them a little shake. They rippled nicely. A tear was flowing down from the girl's right eye. She had done a lot of crying. So did most of the other cunts. In the beginning, it had bugged him and he had tried to make them stop. But that just made things worse. You just had to accept it; girls cried a lot. He found that it was better that they let it out. After, they became more accepting.

He wanted to fuck her again, but thought that he should get her to eat first. She needed her strength for tonight. His plan was to drive only at night. This made it harder to spot the car. And it was dark inside the car so people outside couldn't see whether the girl was balling or not and she couldn't make signals to people to help save her.

He let go of her nipples, watching the breasts spring back into their normal position. Then he got up and got a can of baked beans from the bag. The stew was for him. He needed the energy more than her. And it was better that she be kept just a little undernourished. It helped make them passive.

The bean can wasn't a pop top so he had to rummage around the drawer for a can opener. He found one and opened the can. The girl was watching him warily. He got out a bowl from the cabinet and poured in the can of beans. He brought it over to the table and set it down. Then he sat back down in his chair and leaned over. He took hold of the duct tape around her mouth and slowly pulled each strip off. She whined as it tore at her skin.

When he had it all off, he put his fingers in her mouth and leveraged out the rubber ball. It had been a perfect fit. He put that down on the table too.

She shook her head and exercised her jaw and mouth. Her eyes were watery. She looked like she wanted to say something, but she didn't. That had been the whole point of the exercise and he was glad that she got it.

"I'm not going to ask you if you're hungry," he told her. "Frankly, I don't give a shit. But we've got a lot of driving to do tonight and I want you to keep up your strength. So I want you to eat everything in this bowl. And I don't give a fuck whether you like beans or not. You'll eat what I give you and like it."

He put the bowl down on the floor a couple of feet away from her chair. "Eat it," he said.

The girl looked at him quizzically. She started to say something then stopped. The tears came back. She squirmed in her seat. Her face grimaced. He could tell that she was dying to say something. He got tired of waiting.

"If you're not down on your knees in a split second with your face in that bowl I'm going to beat you silly." He reached out and grabbed her nipples again, this time pinching them hard and twisting them. The girl's shoulders hunched and she gave out an agonized whine.

He pulled her to her feet by her breasts and led her over to the bowl. "Get down and eat!" he said curtly.

Tears were running down her face. She sank to her knees. She leaned over so that her face was over the bowl. She gave him one last look, one mixed with hatred and shame, and then she did what she was told.

She started nibbling at first, licking up a few beans here and there and swallowing them quickly. "She's going to take all day," he said to himself. He squatted down, took hold of the hair in back of her head and pushed her face down in the mucky beans. He mushed it around so that it got all covered. She squealed and blubbered. Then he pulled it up. "When I say 'eat!', eat!"

Her face was covered with brown sauce. Here and there a little baked bean had adhered to it. The sauce was dripping off her nose. He reared his hand back and gave her a powerful slap on her buttocks. She screamed, "Ohhhhhhhhwwwwwww!"

"Get going or you'll get another!" he yelled.

Crying, she dipped her head down and took a mouthful of beans. She raised her head to chew it. The sauce was dripping from her chin. It was running down her throat and down over her chest. When she finished the first mouthful, she leaned over and took a second. Then he sat down and lit a butt.

While he smoked, he watched her eat. Making them eat from the floor like dogs was the best way he knew to teach them what pieces of shit they really were. When you came right down to it, they were barely human, and only really necessary to fuck and make babies. And clean and cook too, though, when push came to shove, men could do that too.

Carly was way beyond hysterical. The man frightened her so much it made her bones sick. She knew that he was doing it to humiliate her, but knowing that didn't make the humiliation any better. They were going to drive all night. She would have to spend another day with him. She didn't know if she could stand it. But she knew that she had to. She had to do whatever he said. Her rear end burned where he had slapped it, and that was only a miniscule example of what he was capable of. Besides, she knew that if she became too much trouble, he would just kill her.

She ate and ate and ate. She could feel the sauce running down over her chest and breasts. She hated beans and was too upset at her plight to be hungry. She knew though that she had to eat it all, a whole can's worth, or he would strike her again. When she was done, she licked the plate clean just for good measure.

He had finished his coffee. When she had finished licking the bowl clean, she knelt up and looked at him expectantly. That was a nice touch. She learned fast, he thought.

He got up from his chair and stepped over to her. He took hold of the hair at the back of her head with his left hand and then leaned over and picked up the bowl. He pulled her to her feet, putting the bowl on the table. He then frog marched her over around the bed to the bathroom. She was a fucking mess. He couldn't fuck her like this. Once in the bathroom, he pulled back the blue, fish strewn shower curtain and made her step into the tub. He positioned her under the shower spigot and turned on the water. Leaning over, bringing the girl's unhappy head with him, he flicked the lever that made the water go to the shower. He pulled her up. The shower spigot sputtered a few times and then the water came pouring out.

It was cold and the girl screeched and struggled. He had a good hold on her hair though and he was able to hold her face under the flow until it was clean of sauce. Then he pulled her back so that the water could get at her neck, chest and tits. She squawked the whole time. Her voice echoed off the brand new, blue tile. But he had to give her credit, she didn't speak.

He used his hand, rubbing it over her tits and chest to make sure that all the sauce was gone. He saw that some had gotten into her hair and he twisted and turned her head so that was washed away too. By then the water had gotten a little warmer so her squawking came to an end.

Still holding her by the hair, he pulled her out of the tub. He released her hair and used a towel to dry her off. She was shivering and crying again. They would take a proper shower later. He didn't want her to get all stinky. This would do for now.

When he had finished drying her off, he took hold of her hair again and led her back to the bedroom. He told her to get on the bed. He joined her.

He made her turn around and untied her hands from behind her back. Then he tied them off in front and affixed them to the headboard like last night. She was forced to lie on her back in the middle of the bed. He drew off his boxers and lay down next to her.

Giving a bitch a cold shower wasn't the best way to warm her up for sex. So he knew that he was going to have to be a little patient if he wanted her nice and hot when he fucked her. He knew a good way to do that.

She was looking up at him, frowning. Her lips were trembling. He was on his side, next to her. He grabbed her hair again, this time not so harshly. "Open your mouth," he told her. When he leaned down to kiss her, her lips were obediently parted and his tongue slipped right in.

He kissed her for a long time. He was on her left and his left hand slid over her chest and her breasts, warming them up. He squeezed one breast, and then the other, not too hard, but enough so that he demonstrated his ownership of them. Her body had been stiff and tense when he first started kissing her, but it was gradually growing softer and softer. He knew she was fighting it, but that wouldn't matter in the end.

When he felt that he had broken the ice, so to speak, he removed his lips from hers and began kissing and licking her neck. She didn't resist him, but he could tell that she didn't like it. His hand drifted down over her belly and across her thighs and then up again. Her legs were together, but he was able to caress her lower belly, just above her sex and then bring his hand up again. He loved the feel of her smooth, youthful body. His cock was hard and his lust was starting to build. You couldn't rush these things though. He had to be patient.

Lowering his head, he took possession of her nipples with his lips. He suckled them gently, running his tongue over them, kissing them. He could tell that she liked this a little better. Even so, she was still fighting him. He took hold of a breast and squeezed it, harder this time while he suckled, kissed and licked at her teat. She shifted underneath him like she was trying to fight something off. When he did the other one the same way, her chest rose and fell and she issued an involuntary sigh. He kept kissing her teats while his hand flowed over her belly again, over her thighs and back. He lifted his head. "Spread your legs," he told her.

She couldn't move her left leg since it was up against him, but she obediently opened her right. Just a little though. He took hold of a teat and twisted it. "Wider!" he ordered. She groaned and obeyed.

"Don't fuck with me, bitch!" he told her. "Just do what I say!"

Her face winced.

He released her teat. Now he would have to start all over again. He brought his head up to her face and kissed her again. He didn't have to tell her to open her mouth, she did it obediently. His tongue mingled with hers, teasing it, playing with it. She began to melt again almost right away. When he was satisfied, he began working his way down her body again. This time, when he put his hand down there, her leg was open and he was able to run his hand over her pussy. He took a finger and dragged it upwards the length of her gash, happy to find some nascent moisture.

The heat of her body was tantalizing to him. He was having a hard time resisting just slipping between her legs and forcing his way in. But that would just make her scream and would wound her insides, making it harder to get a good fuck later. They had a couple more days to spend together. It would be difficult to replace her, and dangerous. So he had to make her last.

His mouth on her teat, he slipped his finger up and down her slit a few more times. When he touched her clit, she gave a little jump. That told him that his magic was working. Blood had started to fill it and it was becoming sensitive.

Satisfied, he began to work his mouth down her torso. His body slipped down the bed while he kissed and licked at her belly. It shuddered when he ran his tongue across it. His hands were on her sides, and they slid down with him as his mouth found her lower belly. She shifted her hips and gave a moan. Her legs twitched as if she wanted to bring them together. He knew that she had probably realized what he was up to and was none too happy about it. That made it all the more delicious.

He scrunched his body down so that his face was level with her loins. He placed his hands on the insides of her soft, white thighs and pushed them apart. She groaned unhappily. He lowered his face, stretched out his tongue and gave her a lick, going upwards, the length of her divide.

She issued a deep sigh. He did it again, and her hips shifted. He did it again, probing deeper this time, and wriggling it just a little and he felt her body soften and heard her breath exhale.

That was all he needed. He kept his hands on her thighs, rubbing them softly while he serviced her crevasse. He licked up and down. He ran his tongue over her clit. He licked the sides and all the way down to the very bottom. He dragged his tongue up and buried it deep inside her now gushing tunnel. He spread his tongue wide and lapped at her love bud and then tickled the spot inside her right at the top. He got a good reaction from that so he did it a few more times. She groaned and her hips twisted. Her legs were spread widely now, of their own volition. When he began to suckle her now rigid love button, her hips rose, her back arched and she moaned deep and loud.

"Ohhhhhhhhh, god!" Carly called out in her mind. When the man had begun to kiss her belly, she knew it would come to this. His tongue and lips were driving her mad. Without thinking about it, she had raised her knees and spread her legs as wide as they could go. It was just like last night. She wanted to drive the hungry lips and rabid tongue away from her, but she had no means to do it. It was like an evil spirit had taken possession of her down there and was burrowing deeper and deeper into her, producing agonizing, persistent, intolerable sensations of pleasure.

She could close her legs and squeeze them tight, making his task more difficult, but he had already shown her how he dealt with resistance. She had no choice but to bear it. The tongue kept licking and prodding. The hands on her thighs, strong, hot hands with amazing sensitivity, were making her dizzy. She bit her lip. There was a part of her that wanted to just give in. "Relax and enjoy it." That was the expression she had heard some men use. Piggish, insensitive men who had no conception of what it meant to be used against your will. She knew that if she didn't fight back with all her determination and strength to resist the blandishments the man's mouth was giving her, she would regret it later. She would be a whore then, a slut, just like her breasts had accused her of being in the mirror. She needed to preserve some of her pride even though and in spite of the fact that she knew that he efforts were doomed to failure. Just like last night, her pussy was in rebellion against its mistress. It had changed sides.

He began to suckle on her clit again, his tongue wagging back and forth on it rapidly. "Ohhhhhhh-hhhhhhhhh!" she moaned. "Ohhhhhhhhhhhhhh!" and she hated herself for it.

He had heard her moans and knew that he had won. It was much more than fun to have a woman in heat at your mercy. He led her up the ladder of lust, making her hips squirm and making her moan deeply, and then he eased his ministrations, letting her slide back down, hearing her groan of disappointment. Four times he brought her to the very brink of completion, four times he brought her back again. She was crying now in frustration and need. Her legs shuddered and her hips ground against his face. The taste and aroma of her arousal was engulfing him like a powerful drug. His cock was like a rock and he wanted to put it someplace warm and wet, but not just yet. He wanted to make her beg for it, to plead for it, to overcome the very lesson he had taught her about remaining silent. It would be a good lesson. He was the master of how she felt, of what she experienced, and without him, she was nothing.

She moaned, she cried, her body twisted, turned arched. And then he heard it. It started like a hum, "Mmmmmmmmmmmmmm! Mmmmmmmmmmmmmmmm! Mmmmmmmmmmmmmmmmm!" and then, like a dam bursting, she screamed, "Please! Oh, god! Please! Please let me come! Please! Ohhhhhhhhhh! Pleeeeeeeease!"

He had been teasing her clit with his tongue, giving it little tiny flicks. He quickly sucked it into his mouth and began to pull on it, sucking at it like a tit while his tongue washed over it again and again. "Ahhhhhhhhhhhhhhhh!" she screamed. "Ahhhhhhhhhhhhhhh! Ahhhhhhhhhhhhhhh!" She bucked and writhed and moaned and cried out. He wrapped his arms around her thighs to better control her as he continued to agitate her point of pleasure. She gave one last, long cry of ecstasy and then her body collapsed.

He suckled and kissed at her sex while her orgasm wound down. He licked its length several times, each time receiving a nervous jolt of her body as a reward. Then he eased his mouth off of her, rearing back his head to view her body.

Her belly and breasts were shiny with sweat. Her face was melted. Her chest was rising and falling laboriously. Her sex was unfolded widely, slick with moisture red and pink. Her little hole gaped in the middle surrounded by tender, glistening flesh. He ran his hand across her belly and it flinched in response. He brought himself to his knees between her legs. He addressed his cock to her dilated, inflamed entrance and slid himself in.

She moaned when he entered her. It was a weak, hopeless moan of protest. But it was all about him now. He had brought her to a meek state of helpless surrender. Now, he could fuck her all day if he wanted.

He slid himself back and forth slowly, reveling in the heat and softness on his cock. He was in no hurry. The abrasion between his rigid staff and her cavern's warm, welcoming walls sent mellow waves of pleasure throughout his body. It was like a favorite sound, or a most delicious taste, and as long as he continued his slow and steady stroking of her cunt, he could maintain it and wallow in the pleasure it produced. He hooked his arms under her thighs and raised them, pushing her knees against her breasts and gave her long, deep, male thrusts. Her eyes were befogged, her mouth pursed, her body slick. After a while, she bit her lip and her face tensed. Her hands formed into fists in her bindings and her body began to shudder. He could feel her pussy contract on his cock. She was coming, but the pacing of his strokes, soft, slow, tantalizing, had produced in her not the consciousness obliterating explosions she had endured moments ago, but a series of ecstatic waves that flowed through her like a mighty, but slow moving river.

He maintained his pace for a long while, shifting rhythms, moving her legs up and down, alternating strokes. His pleasure was like an exhilarating buzzing in his brain. "This is fucking," he thought. "This is worth the world."

She orgasmed again and then again, her body shuddering lightly, her eyes rolling back, her lips quivering.

Suddenly, as if he had achieved a kind of launch velocity, he began to accelerate his thrusts. He raised her knees again and leaned over her. He took her mouth and slithered and slid his tongue over hers. Each time his cock rammed home, the girl gave out a little grunt. It got louder and louder as his motions became faster and harder. He felt his orgasm rising, rising, rising until it became the most important thing that he had ever done to achieve it. All those years of deprivation, the suffering, the lonely nights, the brutality, the cruelty, all were, for the moment, decades and eons away in the past. He was pounding away at her hips now with wild abandon. She was groaning and moaning as he kissed her, pressing her lips firmly against his. Her hips were thrusting back violently. Then, like a bull exploding from a shoot at the rodeo, his orgasm exploded. He groaned loudly. His mind became liquefied. His body felt like it was expanding to the fullness of the room. It was like he was riding that bull and it was jolting and shaking and spinning him round and round and would never stop. She was coming again too and her moans and screams permeated his consciousness like a fierce spirit, egging him on.

And then, it began to fade. The bull slowed. Its bucking wound down. The crowd of enthusiasts that filled his mental rodeo stadium cheered and roared their approval of his prowess. To please them, he gave the girl one, two, three more mighty thrusts for their enjoyment and then was spent.

Carly's body would not stop spinning. She had never been fucked like that. Never. His body lay listlessly atop her. Her legs felt rubbery and weak. It was difficult to breath. Her pussy kept humming and humming. She felt like if he had gone on for one more minute her mind would have permanently crossed the line into dementia. He was like a devil that had captured her and filled her body and mind with insidious spells. Her feelings of utter completion and satisfaction were tainted by a despair so profound that it permeated her very psyche. Knowing that he could do this to her, against her will, made her feel so powerless, so helpless, so shamed, she knew her view of herself would never be the same. Her construct of pride, confidence, independence, self worth and fulfillment had been shattered into a thousand pieces that lay all about her on the bed.

The soothing, enriching and yet passionate series of orgasms he had given her had been mesmerizing. But they were bookended by powerful, soul shattering convulsions that were now burned irremediably into her brain. She knew that the man had delivered to her an experience so powerful, so far out on the range of her conceptions, that he had redefined who and what she was. The old Carly, the one who had gotten into the car back at the gas station a little more than 12 hours ago, would not have been able to conceive of what she was feeling now. But she did not revel in her new discovery. She felt like the man had opened a part of her that should never have been revealed, that should have remained hidden, caged, bound in by the constricts of civilized society. She hated what he had done to her, even as her body lay suffused in the lingering pleasures of what he had forced out of her.

Jack slowly came back to consciousness. Her body was hot and slick beneath him. Her chest rose and fell laboriously. He could feel the beating of her heart. His cock had slipped from its temporary and rewarding home. He slid off her. His body was filled with the torpor that follows release. He needed to sleep. He had duties to perform first though. He crawled off the bed and retrieved the instruments of the girl's confinement. When he returned, he crossed her listless ankles and tied them off. He lay back down on the bed and presented the ball to her lips. Her eyes were closed and she did not respond. "Open your mouth," he told her. Her eyes opened, looked at him unhappily and she complied. He pressed the ball in past her teeth. Then he lay down, his arm strewn across her body, his left leg over hers and fell asleep.

Carly didn't sleep. Her whole being was filled with self pity and woe. The pressure and heat of his body against hers was a forceful, undeniable reminder of her enslavement to him. She wanted to squirm out from beneath him but knew that if she waked him, he would unleash his vengeance upon her. She cried and tried to stop, but she couldn't.

She was able to turn her head to the other side of the room. She saw the clock on the wall. It was a quarter to 1. There were more than 5 hours until darkness. Until then, this room would remain her prison cell, no, not a prison cell, an alchemist's chamber, one in which self respecting, independent women were turned into mere vehicles of lust. Gold turned into lead. She had never conceived that emotions could be so strong that they could permeate your whole body. The last hour or so had been the most intense experience of her life. And the day was not over. No matter where he was taking her, at least once it got dark and she was driving, she would not be a hostage to his powerful prick and his demonic designs. Until darkness, though, she would be his plaything. He would make her do anything he wanted.

On a normal day, at this time, she would be getting ready to come back from lunch. She worked at a warehouse where they stored and shipped electronic parts. She was a picker, roving up and down the aisles selecting this and that obscure article as per the shipping order prepared by the front office. There were four girls who worked with her, Bonnie, Marylyn, Shakira and Penny. Their boss was a merry old timer named Ike, who had been with the company for over 30 years. He knew every part and exactly what it was for. He could spot a discontinued model right off and often, as he inspected their assembly of products, sent them back to get the revised version.

Today was supposed to be inventory. February 1st. It was inventory the first of every month. She was supposed to be there at 7 instead of her usual 8:30. She knew that Ike would have been disappointed when she didn't show up since the other girls would have to pick up the slack. And he would receive it as a personal affront. Not of his ego, because Ike was not that kind of guy, but to his friendship with her. She knew that he would have called her at home to see if maybe she was sick or had overslept. If she didn't answer, he would call her cell phone, the same one that was lying on the side of the road 200 or so miles away from where she was now. But that's all he would have done. He didn't have Randy's number, probably didn't know he existed. And since the argument she had had with her mother last year, she never gave out her number anymore. They hadn't spoken since.

Randy usually called at lunch time. But he didn't call the office. He called her cell phone. He would probably figure that she had forgotten to charge it. They didn't have a date tonight so he wouldn't miss her. He would be pissed though if she didn't call and say where she was and what she was doing. He was a little jealous. She didn't mind since he had so many positive qualities. He was generous and sensitive. He was strong, but not bullying. He was good looking, but not so much that every girl who saw him would want to steal him. He was bright, loved mushy movies, or at least, for her sake, pretended that he did. He was responsible and had a good job at the foundry that had opened last year using all the latest technology and equipment. He had a degree in engineering and knew how to program and repair the robots that did most of the work. And she loved him.

Her tears had begun to dry up, but when she thought of how much she loved Randy and how much she missed him, she broke out in tears again. How could she ever tell him what the man had done to her? He would never understand. She didn't understand it. If somehow she survived her ordeal, she would feel so unclean, so despoiled that she doubted she would ever be able to make love to him again. She would never want him to be where *he* had been. That part of her was soiled and dirty now and would never be clean.

Then, she remembered that it was probable that she would never see Randy again anyway. This man was going to kill her. She knew that. And she despised herself for each little surrender she made to him to forestall that moment. She was such a coward! She didn't deserve to go back to her world. She had forfeited the right to it by surrendering to this man's will. What was the suffering of pain compared to her whole world? She should have never given in.

She should have let him cut her throat there at the gas station, at least tried to get away. It was just when she saw that sparkling knife, his thumb picking at it, and saw his demented eyes and ferocious demeanor, she had been so filled with fright she had frozen in place. Maybe she could have gotten away. If she had run out of the car and he had missed her, he would never have taken the chance to go after her, not when he had what he wanted right there and could drive away with impunity. But her mind had ceased to function. She hadn't had the time to weigh and sift the options. So her inner nature had taken control, she had acted like the despicable coward that she was.

The man was snoring. He lay heavy on her body like a sack of salt. She wanted to wriggle out from under him, to throw him off. Each point of contact between their skin was a source of offensiveness to her. But she knew she couldn't move. She remembered the slaps he had given her, the punches in the car, the threat to break every bone in her face, and she cringed in terror. She nervously tugged at her hands bound above her to the bed. Her whole body felt sick. She wanted to close her eyes and make a wish and be someplace else. Anywhere. Or if she could just melt away into oblivion under him, that would be okay. As long as she was no longer in his presence, no longer his prisoner, as she regained some measure of freedom. For under his demonic reign she had none. Not the freedom to talk, to eat like a human, to get up and walk around the room, to put her clothes on, to be free of his caresses, his terrible control, to use her hands and even the ability to pee when she wanted to. These kind of things happened to other people. Not to her! Not to her!

Maybe he would sleep the rest of the day, she thought. Maybe he would roll over and she would be able to get her feet and hands untied. If she had the opportunity now, she would run no matter what the ultimate consequence. Now that she knew that she was in a battle for possession of her soul. And he was winning.

She eventually drifted off, not, though into real sleep, but more into semi-consciousness. Images kept floating through her mind, disquieting, disturbing images that she not quite make out. They delivered a tension that made her mind cringe.

When he moved, she sprang back into alertness. He rolled off of her with a grunt and then stood up from the bed. He went into the bathroom and took a piss. Then he came out again and gave her a look, a look of ownership. She wanted to curl and cringe and turn her body away from him, but she dared not. She didn't dare to move an inch. He was so big and he frightened her so. When he was done with her, he would kill her.

He moved off. He went into the kitchen area and took the half gallon of milk from the refrigerator. He took off the cap, brought it to his lips and tilted his head back. He took a long drink, one that reminded Carly of her own thirst. With his head tilted back, facing her, his legs spread a foot apart for balance, he looked so tall. His thighs and arms were powerful. His cock hung downwards between his legs, long, soft and rubbery. She couldn't help but stare at it, the serpent that had poisoned her. When he tilted his head back, she looked away so he wouldn't see her staring at it and get the wrong idea.

"Ahhhhhhhh, that was good," he thought as he finished swallowing the milk. Fresh milk was another thing they didn't get in prison. By the time it got to them, it was days old and bordering on if not actually sour. When he looked at the girl he saw her head turn away quickly. He chuckled to himself. He knew that she had been looking at his cock. Why else turn away so fast? Well, it was her master now and she better get used to it.

He put the milk down on the table and walked over to the bed. He told the girl to roll over. After untying her wrists from the bed, he brought them back behind her again and tied them off. He freed her ankles and made her get up. He brought her over to the table and sat her in her chair.

Carly was glad to get out of bed, but not happy to have her arms tied off behind her again. When he did that, she felt that she had been transformed into another animal, not a human anymore. Humans had hands. They used them to eat and open doors and clothe themselves. If she had no hands, she wasn't human.

When he sat her down in the chair, she immediately, without having to be told, spread her legs widely so that her knees were on the outside of the feet. She leaned back so she could sit straight. "I'm well trained," she thought miserably.

Jack had the same thought. He laughed to himself. He leaned over and took her breasts in his hands and squeezed them. Not for her benefit, but for his. He loved the feel of them. Then he scooted his hand down and let a finger trace the inside of her labia. She gave a little jump. She was still sensitive there. He smiled.

It was time for lunch. He brought out another can of stew for himself, the last one, and opened a can of soup for her. It was chicken vegetable. She needed some protein, but not too much. He took a pot out of the drawer underneath the stove and poured in the soup. He was going to warm it for her. He had his reasons. While it cooked, he took out two clean bowls and put them on the table. When the soup just started to bubble, he took it off the range, brought it over to the table and poured it into one of the bowls. He returned to the stove and, after rinsing out the pot in the sink, put two cups of milk in it. He turned the heat to low.

He went back to the table. He took the bowl of soup and put it on the floor. He sat down in his chair opposite to the girl and pried the ball out of her mouth. He sat back. And waited.

Her mouth turned into a frown. She knew what he expected her to do, but did not want to do it, though she knew she would. Then she reconsidered, wondering whether she should move without permission. She started to move, hesitated, and looked to him for approval. He nodded his head. She got up, knelt on the floor, bent over and began to eat.

"See," he said to himself. "Just like a well trained dog."

He opened his can of stew and started to eat it. It was amusing to watch her. Soup was harder to eat that way than beans, if not as messy. And it was just this side of warm. She tried to lap it up, but it was too hot. She looked at him forlornly and then started to blow on it. It took about a minute to cool enough for her to eat it. Then, obediently, she started up her meal.

She slurped up the liquid part and sucked up the chicken and pieces of vegetable. Her breasts jiggled and swayed each time she leaned over to gobble up some more food. She had to spread her legs widely in order to get her head low enough to put her mouth in the bowl. When she leaned up after taking a mouthful of chicken or vegetables so she could chew it, some soup would dribble from her lips and down her chin. He was done before her and he lit a smoke and continued to watch her. When she had just about finished the soup she lathered her tongue all over the bowl to make sure that she got every drop. "Good girl," he thought. Then she knelt up and looked at him hostilely. Her chest was covered with a greasy sheen.

He got up and got the milk. He poured that into the other bowl and put it down before her, removing the licked clean soup bowl. Her brows furrowed and she hesitated again, but fear won out over pride and she went to work on that bowl too. It was not as hot as the soup had been and she didn't lean up so much then. She just kept slurping and licking. It was funny.

She finished her milk at the same time that he finished his smoke. She knelt back with a little beard of white on her chin. He got up and got a paper towel. After wetting it, he came back to the girl and wiped her face and chest and cleaned off her tits. It was easier than getting the bean sauce off her and they would be taking a shower in a little while anyway.

He had something to do and so he wanted to make sure that the girl didn't give him any trouble. He fished the joint out of the ashtray, cleaning off the cigarette ashes, and lit it up. He brought his chair next to where she knelt and proffered it to her mouth. She gave him a dirty look, but took a toke obediently. She held it for about 10 seconds and let it out. He made her repeat it until the joint was just a little nubbin. He put it out and made her eat it. Then he put the rubber ball back in her mouth.

Taking hold of her hair, he pulled her to her feet and led her back to the bed. He made her lie down on her belly and tied off her ankles.

When he got back to the table, he commenced cleaning up from lunch. He took another pull from the milk jug and put it away. He tossed the empty stew and soup cans in the garbage. He took the dishes to the sink and washed them. There was no drain board so he put a couple of paper towels and spread them across the table. He could have left the dishes for the old man to clean up, but for some reason he didn't want the guy to think he was a slob. He also didn't want to give the guy any special reason to remember them.

Carly lay on the bed, the room spinning. Between eating and the joint, a wave of exhaustion passed through her. At first, she had been pleased that the man at least warmed up the soup. But when he gave her the warmed milk, she realized that he had some other purpose than making her eating experience more enjoyable. She lapped it down anyway, afraid not to. When he had her smoke the joint, she was sure. He had warmed up the food so that, after she drank it, she would get tired as it settled in her stomach. Smoking the joint would multiply the soporific effect. If that was the plan, it was working. She was fading fast. She could hear the man doing something, cleaning up the kitchen, she guessed. She didn't hear him finish though. She fell fast asleep.

When he had finished with the dishes, he turned to check on the girl. As planned, she had dozed off. He expected that she would continue that way for a while. He went over to the bags they had gotten at the convenience store and pulled out a pair of steel grooming scissors, some plastic razors and a can of shaving cream. Snapping a few paper towels from the roll, he brought everything with him to the bathroom. He looked at himself in the mirror.

It was the same face he had seen for the last twenty five years or so. He had always worn a beard and shaggy hair. It was mostly because he liked it. But the other reason was a little more subtle. There were very few pictures of him and even fewer of him, at least since he turned 15, without a beard and long hair. His arrest pictures and the pictures they had of him when he was sent to the joint were also like that. Very few people who were alive today remembered what he looked like clean shaven and trimmed.

He started with the beard. He laid the paper towels in the sink to catch the hairs and began to snip off the longest parts. He was done in a couple of minutes. Then he removed the paper towels and started the hot water. He washed his face with it a few times and he lathered it up. Slowly, but surely, the teenage him emerged, but much, much older. "So that's what I look like," he thought as his face was revealed. He had forgotten. If it was a shock to him, it was going to be a real shock to the girl. She would think that he had switched places with somebody.

When he finished shaving his face, he replaced the towels in the sink and started on the hair. He didn't want the hairs to go down the sink and maybe clog it. When the cops learned that he had been here, and he was sure that they eventually would, they were not stupid, maybe they wouldn't figure out that he had shaved. But if the old man had to clean out the drain, they would for sure.

He had learned to cut his own hair in stir. A guard would watch as he used the tiny pair of scissors they allowed him to use and, when he was done, took it back. But those had just been trims, to keep him from looking like Methuselah. Now, he was going to do more than that. He was going to become Mr. Clean Cut.

He didn't do too bad a job. He left it long enough so that it didn't look like he had had a recent haircut. It was still shaggy in places, but the job would withstand everything but a very close inspection. Especially at night when they would be traveling.

He wrapped up the hair in the paper towels and then made sure that all the strays were herded into the sink. He washed the bowl out thoroughly, running it for a full minute. Then, he looked into the mirror again. "Hiya, Jack," he said to himself. "Not bad," he thought. Except for his prison pallor, anyone might mistake him for Joe Paycheck, a regular dude: law abiding, respectful of womanhood and the flag, a Republican by preference, but registered Independent.

There was one more thing to do. He went out and checked on the girl. She was still in La La Land. He rummaged around and found her dress and then he retrieved his socks and boxers and took everything back into the bathroom. He filled up the bathtub to a few inches with warm water and tossed everything in. He took the bar of soap conveniently provided by the management, unwrapped it and proceeded to soap everything down. They would be traveling in fresh clothes. He didn't bother with the girl's underwear. She wouldn't be wearing any.

After everything was soaped up, he drained the tub and filled it again. He rinsed the garments thoroughly. He had often cleaned his clothes in the sink in his cell. Sometimes, for unfathomable reasons, no clean clothes would be issued for a week or two. You needed clean habits to survive in the joint, especially if you wanted to maintain the respect of others, not to mention yourself.

When he was done rinsing, he emptied the tub and filled it again. The trick was to get all the soap out or the garments would end up stiff and scratchy. On the third rinse, he saw that no appreciable soap had been produced and he was satisfied.

He brought the clothes outside to the bedroom. The girl was still sawing logs. She looked cute like that, especially with her mouth bulged out a bit by the ball inside it. Just a teensy bit of blue appeared between her pearly white teeth. Her hands fluttered from time to time in their bonds. He took a close look at her nails to see if she needed to redo them. They looked okay. He wanted her looking sharp when they left, not bedraggled and worn out like a prisoner. He would have her redo her makeup.

He hung the dress from the crossbar of the window curtain in the front of the room by the heater with a hanger he had found in the utility closet. He hung his boxers and sox on the back of a chair and pulled it over to the heater. Everything should be dry in an hour or so.

Now what to do with himself? He looked at the clock. It was just before 2:30. He lit a smoke and brought the ashtray over to his side of the bed, by the bathroom. The girl moaned in her sleep and rolled to her side, facing him. Her thighs were jammed together and he could see the sparse, yellow forest above her mons. That gave him an idea. If he had shaved, she should too.

He went to the kitchen area and got a bowl of hot water. He put it on the floor by the bed while he went into the bathroom and retrieved the razor and shaving cream. He wouldn't need the scissors; her bush was too light and sparse.

When he came out, he knelt by the bed and pushed the girl over. She gave a start as her bound hands poked into her back. Her eyes were wide with surprise. Then she saw him. She saw that his beard was gone. Her face cringed for some reason and tears started flowing from her eyes. He ignored them and untied her ankles. "Spread your legs," he told her.

Carly had been dreaming, she wasn't sure about what, but she had been a million miles from this little motel cabin. Her eyes sprang open when he rolled her over, not knowing what had happened. When she looked at him, she was shocked. He had shaved and cut his hair.

He looked ten years younger. But he didn't look any less frightful. In fact, he looked more. Before, with his whiskered covering and long, unruly hair, he had been like some form of animal from the forest that had claimed her and dragged her to its lair. His cruelties had seemed natural, like that of a thoughtless, wild beast acting from instinct. Now he looked human. A dark, sinister human. His eyes seemed more beady, her gaze more directed and fierce. His mouth, with its thin lips looked mean and cruel. He somehow seemed more conscienceless, more ruthless, like that dastardly guy who put the woman on the railroad tracks in cartoons. He seemed capable of doing that, of thoughtless, cruel, meaningless murder. A feeling of woeful despair shot through her and she began to cry.

She spread her legs like he told her. Then, at his direction, she spread them some more and lifted her knees. He shoved a pillow under her hips, raising her sex in the air. She wondered, frightfully, what he was going to do to her.

He brought the bowl up on the bed and sprinkled some water on her mature growth on her lower belly. Then he took the can of shaving cream, shook it just a little, and emptied a small pile on his left hand. The girl looked at him wide eyed. He rubbed the shaving cream into her hair until it was a mushy mess and then he began to scrape it away.

Within a short while, all the hair above her slit was gone. It was smooth and tender to the touch. The hair around her opening was a little trickier. He dragged the razor carefully around her labial lips, whisking away all the growth. He pushed her mons this way and that until he got it all, right down to the beginning of her perineum. When he was done, he crouched back and admired his handiwork.

It was so pretty! Her pussy had smooth clear lines surrounding the mysterious, wrinkled interior. It was easy to understand where the expression 'camel toe' had come from. They didn't use to do this in his day, but the young guys coming into the joint would all talk about their girlfriend's hairless pussies. It seemed so defenseless, pure and clean. It cried out for ravishment. He leaned over and placed his hand on her lower belly and then over her denuded love lips. It felt so good! He felt a little stubble here and there that he had missed and he brought the razor back over those spots. Where he had shaved appeared just a little red in spots, the irritation of a place that had never been shaved before. He remembered that she had some hand cream in her purse. He got up to get it.

Carly watched him go. Her pussy felt so much more vulnerable than it did before. There was no reason for it. It was no more or less available than it had been. Maybe it was the casual way he exercised his dominion over it. Like he owned it. And certainly like she had no say in the matter. She tried to visualize how it looked. Randy had asked her to do it once and she had refused. She was a mature woman not some prepubescent teen. She wanted him to treat her like a woman. Besides, it was slutty. She had seen some porn pictures on the internet and the women all had their pussies shaved. She wasn't like them.

But maybe now she was. He had turned her into one of them. And he had widened the separation between their relative status in the scheme of things. She felt so much smaller, so much more at his mercy. He seemed so much more powerful and evil. And she knew that her pussy would be so much more sensitive and responsive where her growth had protected it.

He came back with the hand cream. He let out a dollop on his right hand and smeared it over her lower belly where the hair had been. Then he took another dollop and stroked the lips to her pussy and the surrounding flesh. The cream had been cold, but his hands were hot. She felt her pussy warming. She closed her eyes and tried to ignore it, but that was impossible after all he had done to her. She felt him slide his thumb up and down between her love lips, lingering on her sleeping clit, and then back and forth again and again, slowly, softly until it found its way inside, facilitated by her growing moisture. He sank it into her, plunging it inside deeply several times and then ran it over her clit again which had begun to arise from its slumber. She couldn't help the moan escape from her lips. He laughed.

He left here there while he put everything away. He took the clicker for the TV and punched it on. He retrieved his cigarettes from the table and dug out the bag of nachos he had bought and the liter of Pepsi along with some napkins. He went to his side of the bed, propped his and her pillows up against the headboard and leaned back. Carly kept lying on her back, her hands jammed against it with her legs splayed while he was doing this, too afraid to move without permission. She felt him grab her hair and force her into a sitting position. Then he pulled her across his lap, face down.

His right hand idly caressed the flesh of her backside and thighs while he surfed the channels looking for something to watch. Her rear was raised slightly on his right hand side and her breasts were just outside of his thigh on the left, both equally available. Her legs were spread, giving him easy access to her denuded quim. Carly could just see the TV if she turned her head to the right, and she could hear it without problem. Her skin burned wherever his hand went and she concentrated on trying to ignore the lust stirring sensations.

A voice came on the television.

"...ities are still searching for prison escapee John 'Blackjack' Jackson who escaped from a medical detail while on his way back to Wolverton State Prison yesterday." The announcer was clean cut, a white male, in a grey suit, white shirt and red tie. He was properly officious. A picture of her captor with his black beard and wild hair was shown on the screen behind him, up and to his left. "Two guards," the voice continued, "who had been transporting him were murdered. Jackson was serving a triple life term for murder, racketeering, kidnapping and assorted other crimes. He is very dangerous. Anyone seeing him should report it to the 800 number displayed on your screen. Bill Murphy has the report."

Another voice came on. Carly's body had tensed. A huge pit formed in her stomach. She had suspected that her captor was a cruel and ruthless man and here was the very proof. He had killed two men just yesterday. Two guards! He was going to kill her, she just knew it. She started crying again.

"Thank you Everett," the new voice said. It was a man, a little younger, but just as bland looking as the other. In the background was a visual of a huge, concrete wall with guard towers at either end. The prison. "State Attorney General Preston Baker has authorized a statewide manhunt for Blackjack Johnson. He was the leader of a notorious chapter of the Rouges Motorcycle Club, a lawless group whose activities terrorized the Wausau, Wisconsin area for years. The gang's criminal activity has spread throughout the United States. No effort is being spared, Baker said, to apprehend this desperate criminal. Jackson, 47 years old, was born in….."

The voice droned on. Carly barely heard it. Her body was shivering. She bit down on the offensive ball in her mouth. "He's going to kill me! He's going to kill me!"

Jack was too surprised to see the newscast to turn it off before the girl heard it. Well, the damage was done. Maybe it would make her more obedient, not that she wasn't obedient now. She would know that her very life was in danger, as it was. But that couldn't be helped now. It was three more days to the Mexican border. There was a Rouges chapter in Alamogordo, nearby. That's where he had decided he would go. They did a lot of smuggling of dope and weapons and women back and forth across the border. They would be able to get him into Mexico. Once there, he could hook up with some people and do some earning by running marijuana and illegals across the border and whatever else came his way. They might even let him just lay low for a little while, boning up on his tan and fucking little senoritas.

They had gone about 200 miles last night. That's about all you could do when you traveled at night and had to obey the speed limit. That meant they had another 1,000 to go. That is, if they both went all the way. He would have to see whether she became more of a risk than she was worth. So far, at least from the report, they had not connected her disappearance with him, although that was just a matter of time. With her yellow dress and all, she would be easy to spot, as would her car. Maroon was not an everyday color.

He flicked on a movie. It was one of those action films with that guy whose name he could never remember. He had seen it once in the joint. There were a lot of car crashes and shootouts and a couple of nice looking babes who wore hardly any clothes. He looked at the clock. It was 10 to 3. At 5, they would need to get ready to go. He wanted to run a couple of errands before they hit the road. So he had time to watch the movie and enjoy stroking the now hairless pussy of his slave.

He smoked cigarettes, drank the soda, ate nachos and worried the pussy and tits of his captive. It didn't take long for her pussy to dilate and open, and he was able to thrust two fingers in there deeply, stroking them back and forth and making her moan. He played with her tits with the other hand, when he wasn't snacking, pulling and twisting her nipples, squeezing her breasts. He ran his hand over her smooth ass and down and up her thighs. She raised her head a couple times, once when he was tickling her clit. He told her to keep it down. It was no business of hers what was going on or how he used her. Finally, to get her to stop, he grabbed her clit between his thumb and forefinger and gave it a mighty twist. She howled and her body shook until he let go. She didn't raise her head after that.

The movie ended, like they all did, with the bad guys dead or arrested and the good guys glorified. He hadn't ever met a good guy all his life. The cops back in Wausau were so corrupt they might as well have joined his gang. At least a fifth of their income went to payoffs. Funny though, when the shit hit the fan they all went underground. When they learned that Skeeter had flipped, he called every one of them they had given a nickel to over the years to try and find out where the A.G.'s office was keeping him so they could kill him. Not a peep.

The girl was squirming on his lap, her belly rubbing his cock. His hand was wet with her moisture. As usual, her pussy spread like an unfolding flower whenever it got some attention. And now it was hairless and smooth and it was mesmerizing just to stroke it and feel the soft skin. Her breasts were hard and full with blood. Her teats were stiff as bullets. He felt sorry for this girl's boyfriend. After this, he was going to have a hard time keeping her satisfied. And he would probably have to tie her up and slap her around before she got off. But, then he remembered, she probably wouldn't see the guy again. Too bad. She was a nice piece of ass.

His cock needed attention. He pushed her off of his lap until she was between his knees. He spread his legs wide. Then he pulled her hair until she was on her knees and made her move back a little bit. When she was positioned just right, he pried the ball out of her mouth. Her face was flush with her arousal. He kept hold of her hair.

"Now I've had some pretty good blow jobs since I've been in stir," he told her. "I don't expect you to compete with those. But if you don't give me your best, you're going to suffer. I'll control your head. You just keep sucking and licking. And not too rough either. You touch me with your teeth and I'll pull them out one by one so we don't have that problem anymore, got it?"

The girl's face frowned. She nodded unhappily. He reached down and took hold of her breasts, one by one, and gave them each a mighty squeeze that made the girl cringe and moan, just so she could have a good idea what would happen if she didn't please him.

He pushed her head down by his loins. He was holding his rigid cock with his other hand. She opened her mouth and he guided it in. When it was past her lips, he pushed her head down so that it was all the way in, to the back of her mouth. She choked and gagged. "Now start sucking," he told her.

He leaned back on the pillows and began to draw the girl's head up and down over his cock. He did it slowly, up and down, up and down. She started suckling it and lathering it with her tongue. Her mouth was on the small side and so her cheeks bulged when his cock was all the way in. She kept her lips tight around his shaft. She had obviously had experience. That was good. He hated teaching them.

When the man's cock breeched her lips, Carly thought that she was going to vomit. He would probably kill her right there. She choked and gagged when he pushed her head all the way down on it, but that was only for a second or two and then he pulled it up again.

The sensation of having his meat in her mouth was sickening. She cried soundlessly while he pulled her head up and down. His cock was a vicious presence inside her. If having been fucked by him made her feel powerless and small, this was even worse. All her mind could think was, "Cock! Cock! Cock!" There wasn't anything else in the world but his cock and her mouth. It was salty and tasted of his sweat and, at least in her mind, her own juices. She thought of it having been inside her pussy and now being in her mouth and the thought made her cringe.

She sucked Randy's cock, sure. But that was different. When she did that, she was expressing her love for him and reveling in the pleasure he felt. She always remained in control and never let him place his hand on her head. What the man was doing to her was the epitome of what was bad about sucking cocks. It was impersonal and an expression of his power. He seemed mighty before, but he seemed even mightier now as his cock seemed to fill her whole being. It was huge, thick and long. When he brought her head up ever so slowly, it seemed to be miles and miles long. Her lips were in a big 'O' and it seemed that she had her lips around a mammoth tree.

Her pussy was still burning from his abuse of it while he was watching TV. It was even hotter now. Something about the way that he used her had triggered a deep recess in her soul. Maybe it was because he had driven all self respect out of her. In some twisted way, her mind had convinced itself that because of her fear and abject compliance to the man's demands, she deserved to be treated this way. It was her punishment, justly deserved for her cowardice. Her body now yearned for abuse. Her pussy warmed at being the helpless recipient of his pleasure giving manipulations. It burned at the thought of obedience, of being used by him like the whore she had become.

While on the man's lap, she had resisted as best she could, to no avail, the hands that were torturing her flesh with their hot, capable caresses. When he placed his fingers inside her in a mock performance of coitus, her legs had trembled. She had to jam her eyes shut and bite down on the ball in her mouth to avoid moaning with pleasure. She wanted to come so bad now, that if her hands had been freed, she would have put them on herself, made her pussy hotter and hotter until it exploded. She twisted and turned her hands in their bindings behind her back. If only she could get them free! She needed to come! She needed her reward for her abject submission to the man's demands.

He kept her going a long time. He was in no rush. And her mouth was hot and energetic. He had to say that for her. She had really risen to the occasion. Every once in while, he would stop her, reach under her chest and maul and massage her breasts. She moaned and her body shuddered. Then he would start her off again. The vision of her down turned head, her bound wrists, the semi-globes of her ass, all were exquisitely exciting. He pulled her head back until his cock was almost out of her mouth and ordered her to suckle and lick the bulbous head. When she did it, he leaned his head back and issued a moan of his own. All those years he had yearned for the use of a woman's body, to smell that feminine smell, to have her softness around him. Tonight, when they left, he might be met with a hail of bullets. If he was, it would have been worth it. It would have been a tragedy to die without experiencing this once again.

His need began to come upon him. He had been working his cock with her mouth for almost 20 minutes. His balls were tight and his whole body was electrified. He began to piston it faster and faster. He pushed it deeper and deeper into her throat. She began to gag and splutter. She was groaning and moaning in protest, but he ignored it. A tenseness came over him and he knew it was time. He pressed her head down as far as it would go. His cock exploded. He felt his fluids jetting out from deep within him. Sharp, powerful spasms convulsed him. She was whining and her head was struggling for freedom. "Just a second more! A second more!" his mind screamed. And then it was done. His body migrated into passivity. He pulled her head up and she choked and gasped for air. When she had taken in a lungful, he pushed her head down again so that his cock would be fully encased as it delivered to him little echoing spasms. When they subsided, he relaxed his grip.

Carly was huffing and puffing, trying to recapture her breath. Her heart was pounding. She realized that the presence of the man's cock, his firm hand in her hair, the sensation of her mouth being used as a cunt had caused her to reach delirium. She chided herself for the horrible thoughts that had passed through her head. Somehow, the man's treatment of her was driving her over the edge. She could still taste his cock in her mouth and the sensation of obscene fullness it had caused was still there, lingering, even though she had allowed it to slip out.

She was still bent over, his softening cock just inches from her lips. His hand was still in her hair.

"Who told you to let go of my cock!" the man demanded. Carly looked up at him. His eyes were boring a hole through her. His face was angry. "Put it back in your mouth until I say you can let it go," he ordered.

Suppressing a sob, Carly leaned down, aided by the forceful hand in her hair, and spread her lips around the limp instrument. She took it into her mouth. She shuddered with revulsion. It lay upon her tongue like a dead animal. His jism was still leaking out of it. When he forced himself down her throat, his cum had spurted down it without her tasting it. Now the taste was alive inside her and she cringed.

He left her that way for a while. He lit a smoke and leaned back. He was totally relaxed. He was thinking of Mexico and little senoritas and cash flowing through his hands. He would take a trip to the Pacific and go swimming in it. He might take in a bullfight. He would build up his stash and then move to Costa Rica or someplace, get a little gig going. He was getting too old for this gangster stuff. The girl squirmed between his legs and whined. Her back was probably getting crinks in it. Too bad, he thought. He reached out and slapped her ass hard. "Keep still, cunt!" he told her loudly. "And keep quiet!"

Her warm mouth was a pleasant receptacle for his tired prick. Her tongue moved around now and again and her mouth contracted when she swallowed her saliva. It gave him a little twitch. He couldn't decide whether to wait for it to get hard again and let her suck him off one more time. He looked at the clock. It was a quarter to 4. No, they better get going. It was time for their shower. He took a long, leisurely drag on his cigarette. What a lovely interlude he'd had with this little piece, he thought. He would be looking forward to another day of exercise and discipline lessons tomorrow. That is, if she lasted the night. The minute he heard a broadcast that he had kidnapped her, he would have to dump her. With her blond hair and sweet, young looks, she would be too easy to spot.

CHAPTER THREE

In the office of Police chief Martin Brown, Randy was pleading.

"I know that something's happened to her!" he insisted. "She wouldn't run off this way!"

"Now, Randy," Brown returned, "we've got to take this one step at a time. There are a hundred explanations for Carly's absence from work today. It's only four o'clock. She might have decided at the last minute to take the day off."

"But she would have called in! She would have said something to me! And she wouldn't have taken today off! It was inventory day. She knew she was needed. She left my place last night because she had to be into work early!"

"Calm down, Randy. Sometimes things come up at the last minute. Maybe she got up this morning and said, 'To hell with it! I need a day off!'"

"I am calm," he said to the police chief tensely while he caught his breath. "If she was going to take the day off, she would've let me know. I'm sure of it."

"Randy, I've got my hands full with this escape thing. All my officers are out on patrol looking for the guy. The Attorney General is sure he's still in the area. I've got frantic homeowners calling at the least noise in the woods. The Superintendent of Schools wanted me to provide police escorts for the kids on their way home today. The Mayor's on my ass about all the overtime. I'm sorry, I can't spare any of my officers to go off on a wild goose chase. And I can't accept a missing person's report until she's been missing 48 hours."

"That's bullshit!" Randy spat back. "And you know it!"

"Listen," Chief Brown replied tersely, "I've known you and Carly most of your lives. You both grew up around here. I know her Mom and I know your folks too. If I thought that something bad happened to Carly, I'd be the first one to shout it out. But I don't. You know that she has a little bit of a wild side. Maybe something you said to her last night set her off. Maybe, and I don't want you to take this the wrong way, but maybe she's got another boyfriend. It happens, you know."

"That's not true! You know it's not true. I would know!"

"The boyfriend is always the last to know, Randy. It's sad but true."

Randy sat back in his chair, defeated. She couldn't have another boyfriend, he thought unhappily. "She told me last night that she loved me."

Randy's cell phone rang. He was going to ignore it, but he thought it might be Carly. He pulled it out of his pocket and looked at it. It was Carly! Her phone number came up! He punched the receive button.

"Carly!" he said excitedly. "Where have you been?"

A man's voice came on. "Hi, is this Randy?"

Randy looked at the phone. Who was this?

"Yes, it's Randy. Who are you?"

"My name's Bob. I found this telephone by the side of the road while I was out jogging this morning, about ten miles up from Frawley's Gas Station. It's the first chance I had to call. You're the first speed dial number. Whoever Carly is, I think she lost her phone."

"Thank you! Thank you! Can you bring the phone down to the police station? Right away? And don't handle it too much. We might need to dust it for fingerprints."

"Yeah, okay. I can be there in about ten minutes."

Bob rang off. Randy told the chief what had happened. His eyes grew large. He picked up his desk phone and buzzed his secretary. "Get me the Attorney General's task force on the Blackjack Jackson escape! Carly Walker's been kidnapped! And get me the FBI!"

* * * * * * * * * * * * * *

They were in the shower. The just beyond hot water was flowing down on them He had freed her hands so that he could wash under her arms and every place else. The water made her skin all shiny and slick. He had lathered up a bar of soap in his hands and was washing her breasts and belly. It was like having his own little Barbie doll. She was standing with her back to the shower spigot. Her hair was all wet and sticking to her scalp. Her blue eyes were clear and limpid, with just a little red ring around them from her incessant crying. He had decided that he had enough of that. He had told her so.

She was a head shorter then him. Like a toy. He reached down and washed her belly and then lower lips. He took his time on her mons, making sure that he soaped her up good between the folds of her sex. She had some feminine spray in her purse and he made a note to make her use it before they left. He didn't want to smell a dirty pussy all night.

The girl was giving out little whimpers as he cleaned her. It was sexy as hell. His cock was getting hard again and he tried to think out mentally whether they had time for another round before he went out. He had to get some new clothes. The prison duds were like a big neon sign that said, "Escaped prisoner! Escaped prisoner!" And he needed to get her a new dress. That yellow thing was just too conspicuous. And he needed to stock up on food and such. He would leave her here, properly secured, while he did the shopping. Why risk having her blurt out a cry of help to someone? He would have to kill her on the spot and he very much wanted to spend at least one more day with her. She was a real prize. In the old days, when he ran the club, he might have even kept her around for a while. She certainly had good trade value too. If he got her all the way to Alamogordo, well, he would need something to trade for a ticket to Mexico. Although he was sure the dudes in the local chapter would help him out anyway, it didn't hurt to be able to give a little quid pro quo. He didn't want to be beholding to anyone if he could help it.

He washed her face and then made her turn around. He did her back and then her ass. He made sure he got between the pert little half moons. She flinched when he did her bung hole. It made him laugh.

Somebody had left a bottle of shampoo in the shower and he used that to wash her hair. He massaged her scalp firmly. She must have liked it because her body seemed to relax when he did it. He rinsed her hair thoroughly. Now it was his turn.

He handed her the soap and told her to go to work. They traded places. She tentatively spread soap over his chest. Her hands were a little bony and she had long fingers. But they were very soft. She spread them over his chest and over his shoulders. She was trying not to look at him. He admonished her with a little slap on the back of her head and she then turned her eyes to what she was doing.

When she had finished up above, her hands went down to his belly and hips. She lathered the soap up and then spread it over his abdomen. He was watching her intently. He knew that she was not looking forward to the next part, but he was. She looked up at him furtively and then down at her hands. Then, without further hesitation, she began to soap his sex. "Do it good," he told her. She looked back up again, frowned and then looked back down. Her hands manipulated his cock and balls, spreading soap over them. His cock grew as she was handling it. By the time she was done, it was rock hard. He told her to kneel down and do his thighs, legs and feet.

She slowly sank to her knees. His cock was a couple of inches from her face. She soaped up his thighs, massaging them good and then did his shins. He lifted his feet and she did them thoroughly, even between his toes as he lifted each foot in turn.

He turned around and told her to do his back. She rose from her knees and did from his shoulders to his waist. Then she did his ass. He reveled in the heat of her hands and the delicacy of her touch. Without his having to tell her, she got to her knees and did the back of his thighs and shins, all the way to his ankles.

Steam was rising up all around them. Carly was lost and confused. She couldn't deny that it had felt good to have him wash her. It was like being a little girl all over again. His hands were so big and covered so much of her at a single time that it made her feel tiny. Doing his body was tortuous. She didn't want to get excited, but he was a big, masculine man, more masculine than anyone she had ever met. His muscles felt good under her hands. They felt like they were made of steel. She felt guilty about the pleasure she experienced from washing his balls and cock. She knew that she should have been repulsed at having to handle the weapons that he had been using against her so efficiently, but there was something about having them in her hands that made them just a little less threatening.

When she knelt down to do his thighs, the cock, now hard and rampant, bobbed a few inches from her face. It would have been a simple thing to take it in her mouth. She was surprised that he didn't order her to. A part of her was disappointed. Having his hot, thick tool in her mouth had been a watershed experience. She had hated it, still hated him for forcing her to do it, but there had been something so right about it that she was worrying about herself. She had heard of the Stockholm syndrome. They had studied it in school. She knew that helpless captives often became psychologically attached to their captors. How could you not feel drawn to so much power? And he seemed most powerful when he was in her mouth.

He had made her do it a long time. Her jaw had started to ache and her back too. It had been a difficult position with her knees jammed together between his thighs, leaning over, her bound hands unable to help her keep her balance. His hand in her hair had guided her up and down. All she had to do was keep her mouth a narrow, velvety passage for his cock and twirl her tongue around now and again. When he had made her suckle the end of his cock, she teased the opening with her tongue the way Randy had taught her to do.

"Randy, Randy, Randy," she thought. "Where are you now and what are you doing? Have you figured out that I've been kidnapped? Are you desperately hoping that the police will find me and save me? Do you have any inkling of what the man is doing to me?"

The man told her to do his back. She stood again and began washing it. When she got to his ass, she hesitated for one moment and then covered it with soap. Like had had done to her, he washed inside the long crack and timidly washed the little opening. His buttocks were so hard. His thighs were so powerful. No wonder he could fuck her for what seemed like hours and hours without breaking for a rest. She had received the powerful thrusts that his buttocks were capable of producing. She would do so, she was sure, again. Maybe she should just let it happen. She couldn't stop him anyway. If she were more cooperative, maybe he would be nicer to her. Let her eat at the table maybe. Let her be untied for a while.

She got on her knees to do the backs of his legs. When she was done, he turned around. He got on his knees so she could wash his hair. She massaged his scalp, their faces just inches away. She could feel his breath on her. Her breasts touched his chest. She had to take a deep breath.

Then, his arm circled about her waist. He pulled her to him. Their lips met and they kissed. She melted in his arms. She placed her hands on his hips. His cock was pressing against her belly. She slipped her hand over it. A rush of pleasure went through her. It was so hard and strong. The water falling about them made it slick and she slipped her hand up and down it several times. "Oh, god, what am I doing?" she thought as his tongue inflamed her. "What am I doing?"

Jack reveled in the hand on his cock. She had such a tender touch. Nobody had touched him in that way there for a long, long time. He pressed her body tightly to him.

Something had come over him. He needed this touch of flesh. Their thighs and bellies were matched, her breasts pressed against his chest. Her hand was tantalizing him.

"Enough!" he thought suddenly. He pushed her away, broke their kiss and rose to his feet. His cock was just above her mouth. She didn't need to be told. In a moment, she had engulfed it, her hands on his thighs. He moaned. Her mouth and tongue were bringing him waves of pleasure. He felt her cup his balls with her hand and, with the other one, take hold of the base of his cock, holding it still, giving it slow, soft tugs. His knees felt weak and he placed his hand on her head, not for control, but for balance.

She went on and on. The hot water drummed down on their bodies. He could hear her moans. His blood was rising. Suddenly, he pushed her away. An impulse has seized him.

He turned off the water and brought her to her feet. He stepped out of the shower first, pulling her after him. He dried himself and then her with the coarse towels that old man had provided. He took time to make sure that her hair was dry and then, using the brush he found in her handbag, brushed it until it was straight. Then he took hold of her wrist and led her back into the bedroom. "Get on the bed," he told her. "On your knees."

"He's going to fuck me," Carly thought as she climbed on the bed. The thought did not carry the terror that it did only a few hours ago. She wanted him to fuck her. Needed him to fuck her.

She spread her legs and bent over, her face and hands on the mattress. She realized that her view of what her happened to her had changed. Then, she wanted to escape. Now all she wanted was to stay in this little cottage forever. To fuck and fuck and fuck. He could do whatever he wanted to her. She would suffer all of his indignities. She would eat from the floor, suck his feet, spread her legs for him, open her mouth, do whatever he wanted. All she asked in return was to be driven again and again to that exquisite apotheosis of bliss, to never have to think, to just experience, to have her body shaking and writhing with pleasure. To feel her pussy filled and celebrating with mad joy as he plowed her, fucked her, used her, drove her wild with passion.

She heard him behind her moving around and then he was on the bed. He placed his hands on her back and caressed her trilling skin. She felt so clean and renewed. She had been reborn for him, his plaything, his slave, his idolater. He moved his hand between her legs and caressed her smooth pudenda. She almost fainted with lust. He stroked her, placed his finger along the sweet divide and entered her with it. She was wet and ready for him. A moment later and his cock begged entrance. It probed her opening and then slid in to its length. She groaned.

Jack sighed as he felt himself enveloped with her heat. His hands on her buttocks, he sawed himself back and forth, back and forth, waves of pleasure flowing through him. She was moaning beneath him. He was so hot, he felt his need coming upon him right away. "No," he thought. "Wait. Wait."

Carly felt him slide slowly from her pouch. She resisted the urge to call to him. "Please! Please!" she thought. "I need it! I want it!"

There was a pause. He pushed down on her hips. He spread her ass cheeks wide. "What is he doing?" she thought, confused.

Jack had retrieved the lubricating gel from the girl's handbag before getting on the bed. When he had pulled out, he had covered his long, thick crank with it. He pushed her down to make her nether hole available, spread her cheeks, paused, and then slowly eased himself forward.

Carly felt the thick presence at her rear passage. Before she knew it, the head of the man's cock had breached the entrance. "No! Don't do that! Don't do that!" she screamed inwardly. She felt it go forwards more and her little ring began to stretch. It hurt.

"Please! Don't do that!" she called out, forgetting her place, forgetting his ironclad rule of silence. She hated the idea of being fucked there. One of her boyfriends had tried to do it to her one night when she was drunk and she had turned around, slapped him and kicked him out of her apartment. She had vowed never to do that with anybody. And now *he* was doing it to her. Why? Why? "Please stop! Pleeeeeeeeease!" she called out again.

He heard her entreaty and it enraged him. He reared back his hand and gave her a mighty swap on her rear. "Shut the fuck up!" he yelled. He slapped her again and again. "Shut the fuck up!" he yelled again. He reached around her hips with both of his hands and grabbed her nipples. He twisted them fiercely.

"Shut...the...fuck...up!" he yelled.

Carly whined and cried and twisted her body to try and get the vice like grips off of her teats. "Ohhhhhhhhh! Ohhhhhhhhh!" she called out. "Ohhhhhhhhhhhhh!"

He released her and then leaned back again. Her whole body was trembling. She felt him move forward. She felt her tissues tear and she screamed with the pain. "Ohhhhhhhh! Ohhhhhhhhhhh!" she cried out.

He continued until he was sunk fully within her. "Ahhhhhhhhhhh! That's so good," he thought deliriously. Her ring was nice and tight around his prick. Her murky depths were heating it. He began to saw back and forth, his hands tight on her hips. The pleasure washed over him. The cabin started to spin. "Yes! Yes!" his mind called out.

The girl was sobbing and moaning. Her cries merely served to accentuate his pleasure. He went on and on. He felt his crisis coming and he concentrated madly at keeping it off. He slowed himself until the wave subsided and then he began again. When his need again became acute, he slowed once more until it passed. Then he started again, slow, hard strokes that made the girl's body jerk back and forth.

He could ignore his need no longer. He began pistoning back and forth madly. The girl's cries gained tempo and volume. Then he came, splashing his juices into her bowel. His cock throbbed and jerked and his eyes rolled back. When he had cleaned her little aperture in the shower, he had been reminded that he had not penetrated it yet. He had spent years butt fucking, but hearing the feminine pleas and cries was much different than the low pitched whines and cries of complaint he experienced when he used one of the bum boys for the first time. It was so much more exquisite. So much more satisfying. She had almost got him there in the shower when they kissed. She had almost gotten her hooks into him. How better to remind her of her low, denigrated existence than to use her like this. She was a mere warm encasement around some rather pleasurable holes and it was better that she not ever forget it.

His orgasm reached its peak. He grunted and roared his pleasure. And then it faded. His motions slowed. His body felt the familiar enervation of post coital bliss. His grips on her hips softened. He leaned over her torso and came to a halt. "Oh, that was great!" he thought.

Carly cried and cried. What he had just done reminded her who he was and what he was going to do to her. She recalled bitterly her momentary sense of enthrallment by him, wanting him, needing him. He was a devil! He was evil! She had to get away! She had to! He was going to kill her!

He leaned back and his cock slipped from her. She let her hips fall and she scrunched herself into as small an object as she could make of herself. She sensed him getting up from the bed. He went to the bathroom. The sink began to run and she realized that he was cleaning himself off. He had forgotten to tie her. There was nothing between her and the door. It was her chance!

She sprung up from the bed and turned to the door. She stumbled and fell to the floor. She was up in an instant and had her hand on the brass chain that secured it. It wouldn't move! It was stuck! "Please! Please!" she yelled inside desperately. Then it moved. She slid the bolt down and it came free. She grabbed the handle of the door and turned it. The door began to swing open.

Jack had heard her fall to the floor. For an almost fatal second he wondered what it was. He looked into the bedroom and saw female flesh on its feet and scrambling at the door. His reaction was instantaneous. He leaped over the bed. The door was just opening. She was almost out. He reached out and took hold of a skein of hair at the back of her head and pulled her back. At the same time, with his other hand, he pushed the door closed.

Carly felt his hand in her hair. "No! No!" she screamed. Then her head jerked back and she was tossed upon the bed. She scrambled to get up, but he was atop her. She kicked and screamed and pummeled him, but it was like wrestling with a mountain. He quickly had her down on her back, his hand over her mouth, his knee in her chest. His face was erupting with rage.

"You cunt!" he yelled. He removed his hand from her mouth and gave her a mighty slap. It rocked her jaw. She tried to scream again, but the powerful, open paw came back again and drove itself into her face. "Oh, god! Oh, god!" she screamed in her mind. "He's going to kill me!"

He grabbed the hair on the back of her head and dragged her across the bed where he found the ball he had been using to silence her. She tried to stop him from putting it in, but he grabbed a teat and twisted and turned it until she screamed with pain. The ball went past her teeth and sunk home.

Then she knew that she was defeated. Her body went limp and she began to sob.

He brought her to her knees and bent her over, surrounding her with his body. "You stupid cunt!" he yelled. "This is what happens to stupid cunts like you! This is what happens!" He reared back his hand and gave her a fierce swat across her rear. The he gave her another. And another. And another. Something had snapped in him and he was unleashing his fury on her. He struck her again and again. Carly sobbed and cried and her arms flailed uselessly. The blows made her body shift and rock. It felt like a hundred hornets were stinging her there. He just kept going on and on and on. "I'm sorry! I'm sorry!" she tried to say between her sobs. "Please stop! Please!"

After the twentieth blow, Jack started to get a handle on himself. Her ass was rosy red. His hand was stinging. He had almost blown it. He was thinking with his cock instead of with his brain. The cunt had put some kind of a spell on him. She had to be punished.

He dragged her to the middle of the bed. She did not resist him. He secured her right arm to the headboard so that it was extended and then did the other arm on the other side. She was lying on the bed, her arms full out. He took another rope and tied her ankles together side to side instead of crossed and then affixed them to the footboard. He stood up. His blood was raging. He had almost blown the whole thing. He could just picture her running out naked into the parking lot screaming, "Help me! Help me!" He would have had to jump in the car and drive away. It would probably have taken the cops a few minutes to get here. They would have chased him down and it would have been all over. He would have been shot down naked like a dog. Something had to be done.

He scooped up his now dry skivvies and put them on. He found his pants and the sweatshirt he had lifted yesterday. He put on his socks and boots. From his bulky, beige jacket, he retrieved the Swiss Army knife that he had found in the girl's glove compartment. He put it in his pocket, went to the door and went outside.

Carly watched him go. "Oh, god, what have I done? What have I done?" she worried frantically. She didn't know where he was going, but she knew that it couldn't be good. She tugged and yanked at her bindings, desperate to get free before he came back. Less than a minute from when he went outside, he strode back through the door. He closed it and put the bolt back on. He turned to her, fire in his eyes.

He had in his hand a long switch. He had cut it from a branch outside. "Oh no!" she thought miserably. "He's going to whip me!"

Jack watched the girl's face scrunch up in woeful dismay. She knew what was coming. Well, she had earned it. He had made a lot of threats to her, but he hadn't carried any of them out. This time it was no threat. He was going to teach her a lesson she wouldn't forget.

A sickness flowed through Carly's body. She looked at the evil instrument in the man's hand and cowered. "Oh, please don't do it," she whined in her mind. And then aloud, through the offensive and silencing ball in her mouth, "…eeese on't oo iit! …eeeeease!"

The switch made a blur as it traveled from its position at rest, over the man's shoulder and across her thighs. A line of fire broke out where it kissed her. She arched her back and screamed. She yanked desperately at her bindings, but she wasn't going anywhere. He waited a few seconds and the switch began to travel once more. It landed across her belly. It felt like rough, broken glass had been dragged across it. She screamed again and her body jerked up and down. She saw the deranged look in the man's eyes and knew where the next one was coming. "Please, no!" she begged the cosmos. Her entreaty didn't stop it. It landed across her breasts. She howled and howled. Her face was awash with tears. He brought it down again on her breasts. Her whole body cringed and she howled again. She knew that if he kept this up, she would go out of her mind. "Make it go away! Make it go away!" she prayed desperately. "Make it all go away!"

He landed one more blow to her breasts and then one to her belly and three more to the front of her thighs. The girl's body shuddered and shook and she screamed anew each time that the switch kissed her. He paused. Bright red lines ran across her body in a parallel series. She was moaning and crying and her face had turned bright red from her exertions. It wasn't enough. "Let her spend twelve years in stir and see what it's like," he thought. She had no right to endanger him. Who did she think she was! She was just a stupid cunt! She deserved everything she got!

He went to her legs and untied them. Then he brought them back over her head and tied them to the headboard, exposing her ass and the backs of her legs. He ass was still raging red. It was going to hurt like hell.

He raised the switch and brought it down on her blooming red cheeks. She howled again and her legs swayed back and forth in desperation. He worked his way down the back of her thighs and up again, her howling and screeching through her gag all the way. He gave her ass three more blows. Then he was done.

The room was filled with her dismal sobbing. He found his smokes and lit one. He sat in his chair. He felt drained. All his anger had left. But the feeling that she had betrayed him remained. He realized that she was probably more trouble than she was worth. The main point was to get away, not get laid. Pussy was a dime a dozen in Mexico. He knew that he should probably do her right now. Release her legs and draw his blade across her throat. Then he would leave. The old man wouldn't find her until tomorrow morning. He would be hundreds of miles away.

He looked at the bottle of Jim Beam on the table. He didn't drink, but he felt that he could sure use a belt now. He opened the top and took a deep swig. It burned going down, burned real good. He took another swig and put the bottle down and capped it. A feeling of ease flowed through him. "I've got to think this out," he said to himself. She could still be useful. And fucking her was such a pleasure. He would make up his mind when he came back.

He got up from his chair and went to the bed. He released her legs and let them fall. The girl's sobbing had subsided, but she was still crying. He undid her hands and then flipped her over to her belly and tied her hands behind her back. He needed her secure while he was gone. And he would make it so that she would think long and hard while he was away about who was the boss.

He had tied her hands palm to palm, unlike usually where he just crossed them. It had the effect of pulling her shoulders back. He took another piece of rope and tied one end around her arm just above the elbow. Pulling her arms together, he tied the rope off so that her elbows touched. She moaned in pain. He got off the bed and retrieved the roll of duct tape. Then he flipped her over to her back and put three long pieces across her mouth, sealing in the muffling ball. Her eyes were wide with terror. "Good," he thought.

Pulling her up from the bed, he led her into the bathroom. She had to hop because her ankles were still tied together. He lifted her and put her in the bathtub and made her lie down on her belly. With another length of rope, he tied her knees together. Then he brought up her feet, pulled them up towards her head as far as they would go and tied them off to her hands. She screeched in protest. He stepped back to admire his handiwork.

She was tied up just about as tight as a woman could be tied. She wasn't able to move a muscle. She whined and squealed and tried to look up at him over her shoulder. It would be uncomfortable and get more uncomfortable the longer she was there. That was the whole point. Maybe she would be good after this. He had showed her what could happen. It was all her fault.

He went back to the bedroom and pulled a pillowcase off of one of the pillows. Back in the bathroom, he draped it over her head and tied it off around her neck. Not so tight that it would choke her, but tight enough so that it wouldn't come off. It would deaden her moans and squeals, although she would have to squeal pretty loud to be heard through the duct tape. She would not be able to move from the position he had placed her in. She would have to overcome the smooth sides of the tub and that would be impossible. Barring the intervention of some independent force, she would be right where she was when he returned, no matter how long it took.

It had just started to get a little dark outside. He turned on the floor lamp by the bed and then the TV. He turned the volume up. The car would be gone for a while and he wanted the old man to believe that someone was still there. It would also cover up any faint noise that might come from the bathroom. Girls could wail real loud when they were unhappy.

He went back to the bathroom. She was moaning. Her body was vibrating violently. She hardly made a sound. He shut out the bathroom light, leaving the fan on to mask her limited noise, and closed the door.

* * * * * * * * * * * * * *

He knew exactly where he was going. He had spotted it on the way in last night. Of course, it had been closed then. But now it was open.

As he pulled into the army navy store parking lot, a light green Chevy Trailblazer pulled out. There were no other cars in the parking lot. He drove around towards the back and saw a red, late model Sonata parked there in what he presumed was an employee's spot. He drove the maroon Malibu to a slot towards the side of the front entrance and parked.

The building was stand alone. There were no other stores near it. Behind it was just woods and woods a hundred yards on either side. It was perfect for him. Not that he was looking to knock the joint over or anything, but if something did happen while he was inside, like some kid pointing at him and saying, "Mommy, isn't that the man who was on the TV today?" he would be in a better position to deal with it than if the store was in a strip mall.

He stepped inside. The store was called 'The Rack', and sold all kinds of army style clothing such as camouflaged pants and combat boots. There were all kinds of outdoorsy things, like hunting jackets, waders, even tents and sleeping bags. The store carried some women's clothes too. There were denim jumpers and miniskirts, as well as some tops and accessories. It also sold guns. As Jack walked in, he passed a cabinet full of Glocks and .45 Magnums. He tried not to look at them. He had been thinking that it was too bad he didn't grab one of the guards' police issued 9 millimeters when he had the chance. He had the money to buy one, but to get a gun legit, you needed at least a driver's license, something that he was just plain out of. And he wasn't about to steal one since that would bring the entire State of Wisconsin down on him.

He passed by the handguns and headed for the men's clothes. He picked out a pair of green cargo pants and a pair of black combat boots. As he was trying on the boots, the store clerk, who had been sitting behind the counter where the pistols were kept reading a magazine, decided to come over. He was a mid sized guy, in his late thirties, with a more than slight beer gut and hair that had lost a lot of comrades over the years, and was struggling to subsist with the few survivors. He was wearing a Brewers jersey with Sal Bando's name and number on it.

"Those are good boots," the guy said.

"Mmmmmmmmmmm," Jack replied. The last thing he wanted was to start a conversation with him.

"We sell a lot of 'em," he continued. "They were on sale last week. If you want, I could give you the sale price."

"Sounds good," Jack replied.

"Those boots you've been wearing don't seem too worn," he pointed out, referring to Jack's state prisoner issued footwear.

"Don't fit right," Jack replied. He was lacing the combat boots to the top, looking away from the guy. He didn't want to give the guy any reason to remember him.

"Yeah," the man said, "too bad you can't return 'em."

"Yeah, too bad," Jack returned. He really wanted to tell the guy to go get fucked, but that would just cause problems. In the joint a guy like that would have never have had the balls to talk to him.

"Course," the guy continued, "they might take them back down at the state prison. The pants too."

Jack's head snapped up, alert.

"Oh, I don't mean nothing by it," the guy said. "My cousin did a stretch for check fraud. He came back in them same clothes. Got rid of 'em as soon as he could. Just like you. I mean, it's only fair, isn't it. You did your time. Why should you have to go around dressed like some guy who might've escaped from state pr...."

His voice trailed off at the same time that Jack stood up, the surgical saw in his hand. He was at the guy's throat in a second.

"Oh, gosh! Oh, jeeeze! I didn't mean nothing! I don't know who you are! I won't say nothing!"

Jack had the knife to the guy's throat. "Shut the fuck up!" he hissed. "Come with me!"

He took hold of the trembling, whining man by his shirt collar and led him towards the rear of the store. There was a storage area in the back. Jack came out alone a minute or so later. He wiped the blade clean on a t-shirt on his way back to the front of the store.

On the door, the sign said that the store closed at 6:30. It was 6:15. Jack decided to chance closing the store rather than having to risk killing again. Once was enough. Three men in two days. He hated killing. It always left a sour taste in his mouth and sometimes he dreamed about the people who he'd sent on. There weren't all that many, at least not personally. Maybe twelve, if you didn't count these three. And most of them had been guys. Guys on the make who got greedy or who didn't deliver. Guys who had gotten arrested and were cooperating with the cops. He had done two women. The first had been an innocent bystander to the killing of a guy who really deserved it. She had just popped around the corner when he had just finished twisting a 7" long blade in the guy's insides. He had had to chase her down and slit her throat. She was older, maybe in her forties, and a little heavy set, so she didn't run too good.

That had been when he was just starting out, making his bones. The other was he had to take care of this cunt who kept running away from this place where the gang had her spreading her legs for the club's benefit. The leader at the time, a guy named Drummer, whose real name was Cal Drummond, had ordered her taken care of in a very public way so that the rest of the girls would get the message. He and this guy Jed, took her out to the woods and he strangled her. Jed refused to do it. The girl cried and whined and pleaded. She was a looker too. They dumped her body where the cops would be sure to find it. Sure enough, it was headlines for a few weeks. None of the girls ran away after that for a long, long time.

He thought of that girl a lot when he was in stir. He was sorry for having done it. That Drummer was an ass and didn't last out the year. Some Pagan killed him in a bar fight in Muskego. There was a lot of bad blood between the two gangs for a while after that. But eventually, there was a sit down and it all got straightened out. It was a Pagan bar after all and Drummer had no business being in there and shooting his mouth off. Jack was elected Chapter President right after that.

No, he took no joy in killing. But he couldn't take the chance with this guy. He could have tied him up, but he probably would've gotten free eventually. And he would have known what clothes Jack had bought. And he would have known about the cut hair and the shaved beard, although the cops probably guessed that already. The guy had to go. There was nothing else to do.

He locked the door and pulled down the shade. He turned off the light on the sign outside. Grabbing a cloth from behind the counter, he wiped everything he had touched. If the cops didn't trace him to the killing right away, it could save him hours, maybe a day. He put his old clothes in a plastic bag and put on some gloves.

There was about $800 in the register. But in the safe behind the counter, Jack hit the jackpot. The door had been left open so that the clerk could put today's receipts in it before he closed up. There was $5,700 in small bills. Jack put it in a shopping bag and then in the larger one where he had tossed his prison pants and boots. The display case with the handguns was locked. Rather than go back and get the key from the dead guy, Jack smashed the glass with a hatchet. He loaded up a duffle bag with all the pistols in the display case plus ammunition. He stuck a Walther P99 into one of the pouches on his pants along with two extra clips.

Since he had already killed the store clerk, Jack figured he might as well outfit himself all the way. He gathered a sleeping bag, a two man tent, a small gas stove, a large bowie knife in a leather sheath, the hatchet and some cooking gear. He added a couple thermoses and a few more odds and ends. He felt like he was on one of those game shows where you had to gather as much crap as you could from the store aisles before the bell rang. On the clothes side, he added some more underwear, t-shirts and some more socks.

He stopped by the dress rack. What was he going to do with the cunt? He still hadn't made up his mind. Well, if he didn't get anything for her to wear instead of the yellow dress, and he decided to keep her along for a day or two, he would be sorry. He gathered a couple of denim miniskirts that looked her size and a few t-shirts. He also got her a dark blue parka to replace the one she had now. He got a dark green one for himself.

"Shoes," he thought. The only shoes she had now were the canary yellow pumps. He got her a pair of ankle high workout shoes and some white socks. "That should do it," he thought.

He loaded the stuff into the car. The Malibu had a lot of trunk space and he was able to pile most of the stuff towards the back and leave a little room up front for emergencies. He closed the trunk and went back into the store. He double checked to see if there was a burglar alarm to turn on, but he couldn't find one. He locked the front door from inside and then went around the back. As he walked through the back room, he could smell the odor of the man's spilled blood. He made careful that he didn't get any on his shoes and stepped out the back door.

* * * * * * * * * * * * * *

Attorney General Preston Baker was presiding over a meeting of the task force he had assembled in response to the Blackjack Jackson escape. He had been assured by the prison authorities that they would have him captured within 24 hours. It was now well into the second day and the results so far were butkis. They hadn't even recovered the Ford Eclipse the guy had escaped in. This morning, the Deputy Warden in charge of the search assured him that Blackjack was still within 50 miles of the prison.

"We've got this area sealed off tighter than a drum," the Deputy Warden said. "Not even a fart could escape."

"That's reassuring," Baker replied doubtfully.

"All the main and secondary roads have been cut off. I can assure you that the car is somewhere within the search zone." It was the Chief of the State Police speaking. "And my men have instructions to shoot first and ask questions later."

"But what if he made it outside that 50 mile area? Suppose he got hold of another car and drove by one of your checkpoints at night? What then?"

"We'd have heard something by now," the Chief told him. "My guys are keyed into every crime report in three counties. Nothing indicating that our man has stolen a car has come up."

That was at 10 a.m. Now it was a little after 6 p.m. and the men in the room were looking pretty grim.

A snazzy State Police lieutenant had a blown up map of the state on an easel and was pointing at it with a long aluminum thing that folded up and you could stick it in your shirt pocket.

"Here's the presumed point of capture," he stated, pointing out the approximate location of Frawley's Gas Station. "The phone was found a little over 10 miles north of there. We have surmised that Jackson is headed back towards the Wausau area where he has many contacts. Once there, he can connect with a number of potential remote hideouts. He is a known woodsman and could probably last the whole winter out there by himself with just a knife and some warm clothes."

AG Baker looked at his assistant. He had done some checking on the girl's bank account and on her credit cards.

"This confirms the information we have," the assistant stated. "Several withdrawals were made at the Green Mountain Bank and Trust facility in Halleyville. A credit card was used about 12:50 this morning at a Shop and Go convenience store abut 20 miles further north. I'd have to agree with Lt. Peterson. He's headed for Wausau or he's probably there already."

"Which means he's gone to ground. Which means that it will take weeks, if not longer to catch him," AG Baker snorted. "I'm sure the Governor will be pleased with this information as well as having to look at that young girl's picture on every national newscast for the foreseeable future. We can only hope that they don't start one of those countdown things, 'Two Days Since Carly's Kidnap', 'Three Days Since Carly's Kidnap' right up to the April primary.

"We still don't know for sure that he's kidnapped her," one of the junior assistant A.G.'s interjected.

"Oh, he's got her all right," the State Police Chief replied. "The boy at the convenience store confirmed it. We're getting the photo from the bank ATM machine now. That should show them together too. What we don't know is if she's still alive."

"I want her picture plastered over every newscast in the state," Baker ordered. "I want a description of her car given to every reporter out there. Somewhere, some member of the public is going to spot it. Then we have him. I want all teams south and west of Halleysville moved up to the Wausau area. I want all air patrols diverted as well."

"But what if he didn't go that way? Suppose he used the charge card at the convenience store as a ruse to make us think he did and then backtracked and headed south or west?" the junior assistant A.G. spoke up.

"That's nonsense," Attorney General Baker spat back. "The man's been in prison for 12 years. He wouldn't know a debit card from a get out of jail free card. He'd have no idea that he could be tracked that fast. He headed up to Wausau, I tell you. Now get the woman's picture out as soon as possible."

The door to the room flew open. In walked a dark suited man with grey hair, a little past 60, trim. He walked with an air of assurance. Following him was a young woman. She was also dressed in a business suit, well tailored. She was attractive and intelligent looking.

"Who the hell are you?" Baker sputtered. "You can't break into our meeting like that! Chief," he said looking at the director of the State Police, "get security on the phone."

"No need to bother with that, Mr. Baker," the gray haired man stated with authority. "My name is Jason Holmes. Special Agent, FBI. I'm taking over this manhunt as of this moment."

"You can't do that," Baker replied spitefully. "This isn't a federal case yet, not until there's been a ransom demand."

"I'm sorry, Mr. Baker. They're your wrong. It's a federal crime to murder a law enforcement officer. In addition, I understand that Mr. Jackson here committed credit card fraud on companies engaged in interstate commerce. That's wire fraud, another federal crime."

"So what do you expect us to do? Go home and play tiddly winks?" Baker replied nastily.

"I expect you to give myself and the Bureau full cooperation. I expect that all information gathered as a result of continuing investigations will be directed to me. I expect that all media inquiries will be directed to me and I expect that all information released to assisting law enforcement departments will come through me. Is that understood? I can get a Federal judge to order it within the next 20 minutes if you like."

Baker waved Agent Holmes off. "You can do what you want. We're acting on the information we've already gathered. We don't need the FBI. We're hot on this guy's trail. I already ordered an all points bulletin on the kidnapped girl and her car. We should have reports coming in within an hour of sightings."

"If you release that information, that young woman will be as good as dead," Holmes replied. "Jackson will kill her as soon as he believes that she is a liability. And if she and her car are all over the news reports, she will be a huge liability."

"Don't be ridiculous!" Baker retorted. "He's got to know that we're going to make the connection between her disappearance and his escape. If there's no news report about it, he'll smell a rat."

"Maybe so. But if her picture is not all over the news, then he won't have a motive to kill her and dump her body somewhere in the woods. He may figure out that we're keeping her kidnapping quiet in order to keep her alive. That's okay. I know that's it's a gamble, but we have to do everything that we can to preserve this girl's life."

"I say that you're handcuffing us, Holmes," Baker protested. "Besides, what help are you going to be to us? We know where he's going. Our men have a lot of experience up near the Wasau area. You guys don't know shit from shinola about it."

"He's not headed to Wausau," Holmes replied.

"Oh he's not, isn't he? We think we know our man pretty good and we believe he's headed to his old stomping grounds. The stop at the ATM machine and the convenience store confirm it."

"You're making a big mistake. I've read your boy's file. He's no knucklehead. He's had 12 years to think about this. The last thing he's going to want is to be trapped between your people and the Canadian border. He wants out of the country, but not to Canada. Dollars to donuts, he's headed to Mexico. And he's going to look for a Rouges chapter that can help him get there."

"It's almost 1,500 miles to Mexico from here," Baker protested. "He's not that stupid. He knows he can't travel that far without being caught."

"Look, he's got one chance of survival. He's got to get out of the country. Mexico is his best bet. He'll travel at night, stay in small, remote motels, or even maybe camp out. There are 8 Rouges chapters from Dallas to San Diego. Or he could go to Los Angeles, Denver or Oklahoma City. They all have Mexican connections and could help smuggle him out. That's where to look for him. That is, if he escaped Wisconsin. My bet is that he holed up somewhere in state today and that he's going to cross the border into Minnesota sometime tonight. You've got the border crossings all covered. Leave them in place and you may be able to catch him."

"You just got done telling us that he's headed south to Mexico and now you're telling us he's headed west," AG Baker replied haughtily. "Make up your mind."

"From his point of view, he would realize that due north and due south are the directions we'd most likely look for him to go. He did head north for a while, but that's only a decoy. He wouldn't have backtracked too far, so he would have either gone east or west. East doesn't help. So he went west. Tonight, once he crosses into Minnesota, he'll head south. Mark my words."

"Well you can get all your little special agent men out there in Minnesota looking for him, Holmes," Baker replied. "We know where he's going and where he probably is already. I'm directing all our resources to that area. If I get my men on the state line crossings on the move now, they can be in place in Wassau in the morning to start an area wide search. That's my plan. If you want to hold back the girl's kidnapping from the news media, that's your business. But I want that directive in writing so that the press doesn't have my ass when the girl is found up in Wausau with her throat slit."

"I can't get my men to the border crossings in time. Your men are in a perfect position to catch him. He has to cross the Mississippi River to get into Minnesota. There's only about 20 places he could cross. You've got to keep your men in place."

"You deal with your men, I'll deal with mine, Holmes," Baker stated flatly. "We know what we're doing."

* * * * * * * * * * * * * *

Carly didn't know how long she had been tied up in the bathtub, but she knew it was a long, long time. She had stopped trying to scream and yell so that someone might come and save her about an hour ago. She had realized it was useless from the start, but she felt she had to try.

She had thought the man was going to murder her when he dragged her into the bathroom after whipping her. At that point, she had almost wished that he would get it over with already. When he made her get in the tub and then lie down, she thought that maybe he was going to drown her in it. But then he tied her knees together and connected her already bound ankles to her wrists. Her shoulders screamed out their complaints. Her back protested as did her thigh muscles. She started to panic that he was going to leave her like this and started moaning and trying to plead for release through her gagged mouth right away. She hadn't seen him coming with the pillow case. He looped it over her head before she knew it. And then he tied it around her neck. She thought for a moment that he intended to strangle her and didn't want to watch her face, and was relieved when he didn't tie it off too tightly. But then she realized that any plea for help she made would be doubly muffled by the addition of the cloth covering. Then she heard the TV go on in the bedroom and then the bathroom fan. Then she knew that screaming for help would be useless. But she had to try anyway.

And, although she knew she shouldn't do it, she was so overwhelmed with the fear of being left alone like this that she yelled and screamed please for him not to do it. She tried to rock her body, pull at her bound arms and legs, swing her head back and forth, do anything to achieve movement. But it was all useless. She could move virtually nary a muscle. The light, which she could see dimly through the pillowcase, went off. She heard the door close and knew he was leaving. She cried and cried and cried.

After that was when she began screaming. She must have screamed for 15 minutes continuously. Her throat became raw. Her blood pressure built up to boiling. She almost drove herself mad.

After that, she just gave up. She cried some more, over being so cruelly bound, about all the things that had happened to her, being whipped and used and humiliated. Her hands seemed somehow like foreign objects to her. They were out of her sight and out of her control. More than that, they, like her pussy, had betrayed her. They were joined together and refused to become untied to help her. What good were they! They were worse than no help, they were a hindrance, since her feet were tied off to them and now her feet couldn't move either. It was her hands' fault. Her rebellious, disobedient, traitorous hands.

She had never known that her body could become her enemy, like her pussy and now her hands had. In fact, her whole body was in rebellion against her, being all scrunched up and helpless, refusing to become untied, refusing to stand up and walk away. Her mouth refused to talk, her eyes refused to see. She was her body's prisoner, holding her captive so that that man, Blackjack Jackson they had called him, that murderer, could work his will on her. She tried to negotiate with it, begging her hands to move, her feet to slip free of her bonds. She tried to wriggle her body up the sides of the tub, but she couldn't gain even a millimeter of height.

She had never been very religious, but she started to pray. She promised God all sorts of things if he would free her. No more sex, at least until she was married. No more smoking pot. No more drinking. Church every Sunday and all the major holidays. She would give to charity, teach at an orphanage, devote her life to serving Jesus, join a convent, go work for a mission in Africa or India like Mother Theresa. She promised that she would do anything that God commanded. Anything. But please, please, please, get me out of this.

When that didn't work, she began to argue with God. Why did he pick her out for this? It wasn't fair. There were lots of worse people in the world. Why didn't this happen to one of them? And why did he give that man so much strength and cleverness? Fixing her up here in the bathtub had been amongst the cleverest things he had done so far. Why were you, God, helping him and not me? Why didn't you smite down the wicked? Why didn't you protect the weak? Why did a poor girl like me have to suffer this way? What good did it accomplish? If it was your will, God, why was that? Did you enjoy seeing people suffer? Did you enjoy seeing them helpless and miserable and begging you desperately for help and crying and pleading and not getting any answer and feeling worse and worse and worse?

Then she forgot about all that. Who cared about God? If he existed, he was a prick who let all kinds of bad things go on that he could prevent.

Her mind started to wander. She could hear the TV in the other room faintly over the ever present sound of the whirring fan. Strange, disembodied voices, talked, yelled, screamed, sang, argued. She really couldn't make out any distinct words. It was like being held captive by foreigners and they were in the next room arguing in their native tongue what to do about you.

And it was funny, too, she thought, that if they were the disembodied voices, she was the disembodied body. She had a useless, functionless body which could no longer be animated by her mind. She couldn't talk. All she could do was float in a strange, dark void where movement was impossible. Every once in a while she would try and twist her wrists free, or spread her legs or wriggle her feet free of their bonds only to break out into tears at the impossibility of it.

One thing that she kept coming back to was the image of herself in this teeny tiny space, all scrunched up, and all that empty free space all around her. First there was the empty space in the bathroom that she couldn't reach. Then there was the space in the rest of the cottage. All those things, her dress and shoes, all the furniture, the tin cans, the rest of the junk the man had bought, they were all out there and unavailable to her. But they were still real and they were still out there. It only seemed like the universe had been reduced to less than a cubic yard.

And then there was the outside. There were trees and the other cottages and the parking lot and the old man, the road that led to the highway and the world. Maybe the old man was walking around even now, checking things out. He would hear the TV on in their cottage and think, "How wonderful that they are enjoying themselves," or some such rot. But he would be out there. Although it seemed that way, she was not the only person in the world. There were hundreds, thousands, millions and billions of people and they were all just right outside the door to her little prison. And of all those million, billion people, there was not a single solitary one who was going to help her get out of this or a single solitary one who cared if she lived or died.

That was when she really hit the bottom. She was so alone. It was horrible. No one knew what she was going through with the exception of her captor who seemed to delight in her suffering. No one knew where she was except for the dotty old man last night who didn't even care if she put down the names of characters in a fifties sitcom as their names on the register. And even he probably thought she was calmly watching TV, eating crackers and cheese and waiting for her boyfriend to come back with the car.

No, she was all alone and she was powerless. Powerless to ameliorate her suffering. Powerless to free herself. Powerless to make the time go by quicker. Powerless to prevent the man from using her and then putting her away like she was some kind of object he had lost interest in. Powerless, powerless, powerless.

But her captor had power. Seemingly inexhaustible, almighty power. His power was here now with her. It was his power that energized the knots that were holding her so thoroughly still. He had frozen her in place by an act of his will. And she had no power but to obey. And the ball in her mouth. It seemed like he himself were present there, a piece of him that he left behind in her mouth, left behind to invade her inner space, the inside of her body occupied by him. And no matter how she chewed at it, pushed at it with her tongue, shook her head or screamed and yelled, she could not dislodge it. It was him, lodged inside her and he would not go away.

It was all so unreal. Yesterday, this time, she and Randy were probably getting ready to have dinner, kissing and joking, as happy as clams. Clams that were totally ignorant of the cruelty inherent in their world and lurking out there in the darkness waiting for them. "This can't really be happening," she would think to herself from time to time. "I can't really be tied up in some unknown cottage in some unknown town, lying face down in a bathtub, hogtied and hooded, gagged, naked, and at the mercy of a homicidal escaped felon. I really can't be. It's just the plot for some stupid movie. It's not real. It can't be real. Please! Please! Don't let it be real!" But she knew it was real and a sense of mind numbing despair would overcome her.

Her failed attempt at escape came back to haunt her. If only she hadn't slipped! If only she hadn't fumbled at the bolt holding the door closed! If only he had taken a few more seconds to react! She would have been out and running as fast as she could. And screaming! Screaming bloody murder, as the expression goes. But no. She had failed. And now here she was, tied up worse than she had ever been before.

She felt like the most dismal of all the dismal creatures on earth. Part of her felt she deserved her suffering because she had been powerless to prevent it. She wanted desperately for it all to end. She wanted to shrink herself into a little speck of dust and go down the drain. She wanted to stop breathing. She wanted her heart to stop beating. She wanted to stop thinking. Yes, most of all she wanted to stop thinking, measuring the passage of her lonely tribulations by the hundredths of a second. Make it all speed up and bring her to the very end. Skip all the suffering in between and bring on death. But for all her wishes, for all her prayers, for all her broken hopes, she was condemned to await all alone for the disposition her captor deigned for her, no matter how long it took or how miserable she became, naked and bound into total motionlessness and silence, helpless to forestall her fate.

She knew he had returned when the TV was shut off. Her blood ran cold. Then the door to the bathroom opened and the light flicked on. She raised her head, fearful and hysterical, and tried to beg him to release her. But the light went out and the door closed once more. She lowered her head and sobbed.

He saw her there. She was still alive. He thought for a moment that she might be dead, strangled on the rope around her neck or suffocated by the pillow case. Half of him hoped that she would be. That would relieve him of the decision he had to make. When he saw her head flailing around and her muffled pleas for freedom, he realized how distasteful it was going to be to kill her. The taste of the death of the store clerk was still in his mouth and he had hardly said a few words to him. The girl was different. She had helped wash away the bitterness of 12 years of captivity. She had restored him to feeling human, restored his manhood. And her body was so smooth and delicious and her mouth so sweet to kiss and her pussy so sweet to be in.

Then he realized that he never had to see her face again. He did not have to watch her agonized eyes staring at him, pleading with him, hear her cries and wails. All he had to do was reach over, close the drain and turn on the water. He would turn out the light and close the bathroom door. He could come back in 15 or 20 minutes and turn off the water. It would all be over. Like turning off a switch.

He couldn't make up his mind. He turned out the light again and closed the door. He would get ready to go first. Then he would decide.

He gathered all their goods. He heated up the last of the coffee and then washed the pot and the inner workings. He emptied the ash tray, put away the rest of the rope. He made the bed. He swept up. He lit another cigarette and sat down to finish the coffee.

He had stopped at a fast food joint on the way back from the army navy store and had bought himself a deluxe double cheeseburger and fries. He bought for her chicken nuggets. With honey mustard sauce. He hadn't been sure she would ever eat it, but again, if he didn't bring her food, that sort of decided the question and he still hadn't made up his mind. He ate his burger. It tasted like shit. He just kept thinking about that girl's sweet, young body and its destruction. No one in the world would ever again hear her moan with pleasure like he did, would look into her eyes as she came, would feel her pussy vibrate with elation around their cocks. And he thought of her silly, little yellow handbag and the picture of her boyfriend in her wallet, her look of unhappy surprise when she first saw him. He was like a wave of misfortune that had been visited upon her.

But he was thinking like a fool. She was just another cunt. She was there to be used and disposed of. Who cared about her useless, 'normal' life. She was like everybody else. You took from them what you needed, what you wanted. If they got in your way, too bad for them.

Her dress was still hanging by the window and her little yellow shoes were underneath it. He had stuffed her discarded nylons into them. He thought of her putting them on the day before not knowing what fate had in store for her. He remembered her doll like face when she was sleeping. He felt like something was twisting inside him. He had never felt this way about a broad before in his life. What made her so special? Was he getting soft? Old? Or maybe, maybe, he was just tired of leading a life of untrammeled wreckage.

He leapt up from the chair. "Fuck her!" he thought. He was going to do her. He swung the door to the bathroom open and flicked on the light. Without looking at her, he leaned over and snapped the drain closed. He put his hand on the handle for the spigot. He began to twist it. The water began to spill out. She was moaning and crying frantically. Her bound hands writhed. Her body shook back and forth. He turned out the light and closed the door. "There," he thought. "It's done." But his hand never left the handle. "Don't be a fool!" he told himself. "You're better off without her!" And then he thought of her lovely body, her brilliant eyes, the warmth of her mouth on his cock, the way she sighed when he entered her.

He couldn't do it. He pushed the door open. The water had risen already to half way up her thighs. She was moaning and screeching, shaking and twisting her head frantically. He crouched down. He knelt on the floor. He looked at her.

He shut the water off and opened the drain. He watched it empty out. When it was all gone, he untied her feet from her wrists and then her feet from each other. He lifted her from the tub. She was sobbing heavily. He took a towel and quickly dried her off. Then he dragged her from the bathroom into the bedroom and over to the table. He let her slip to her knees and untied first her elbows and then her wrists. He took off the pillowcase and then, lastly, removed the blue ball from her mouth. He went and sat in his chair.

Her hands dangled at her sides. Her eyes were doleful and sad. Her lips were trembling. The stripes he had put there still marred her breasts and belly. She stretched and expanded her body to try and make sure that she was really unconfined. She began to murmur something. He couldn't understand it. She was crying, tears pouring down her face, and the words were coming and coming, words that she kept repeating but he couldn't make out. Then she fell to her hands and knees and started to crawl towards him. "I'm sorry," she said. "I'm sorry. I'm sorry."

He was perplexed. Sorry for what? And then he remembered. She had tried to run away. She thought that all of this had been a punishment for trying to run away.

She reached his chair and started kissing his boots. "I'm sorry! I'm sorry!" she was saying louder now. She raised her head and started climbing his legs. He was too astounded to stop her. When she was kneeling between them, she ran her hands over his thighs, her eyes flitting up and down again at his. Her face was wrinkled with her delirious unhappiness. She lay her head in his lap. She was sobbing. Her hands continued to rub his thighs, now along the outsides. Then her hand moved again. She lifted her blond head and her hands took its place in his lap. He felt fingers seeking out the buckle to his pants. They loosened it, separating the halves, and then slowly eased down his fly. Her eyes, red from crying, dark from her agonies, stared up at him cautiously as if waiting for a blow to fall. He let her continue. She fished out his hardening cock. Her hand was hot around it and he issued a sigh of pleasure. She looked at him whispered two more times, "I'm sorry, I'm sorry," and then she leaned over and subsumed his cock into her mouth.

Her lips and tongue consumed him hungrily. Her hand reached into his open pants and cupped his scrotum gently. Her tongue flitted over the tip as she suckled the head. She moved her head up and down, up and down, her free hand rubbing his belly and chest under his shirt. She swirled her tongue around, held her lips fast to the skin of his thick stem, took it to the very edge of her throat and held it there. He moaned and groaned. He sat back in the chair and placed his hand on her head, not for control, but in acceptance of her efforts.

He let her go on and on. She was going good. He held himself back as long as he could. And then he came. Her energies increased fivefold. Her mouth bobbed rapidly, her tongue swirled madly. She squeezed his balls gently and circled the base of his cock with her other hand. She moaned and twisted her head, getting as much moist friction as she could on his cock. He bellowed his pleasure, grabbing her head with both of his hands and holding on to it tight. He felt like he was emptying his whole body out through his cock. It just kept going and going. A flash of pleasure jolted through him at each mighty spasm. Until, finally it wound down. He was out of breath. His heart was pounding. His body shivered with tweaks of pleasure as she suckled his cock to obtain all of his discharge. When he had gone soft again, she laid her head in his lap, flung her hands around his waist and cried.

He let her go on for a few minutes. Then he gently pushed her back. He lifted her head and told her to crawl back a few feet. He addressed her.

"We're going to be leaving in a few minutes. First I am gong to feed you. Then, there are some new clothes I bought for you to wear. You will try them on. Choose the ones that fit you best. Then I want you to put on your makeup like you had it yesterday, lipstick, eyeliner, the works. Then we'll be going. We'll be driving all night. Tomorrow, we'll rest again. Do you understand?"

She nodded her head, her face neutral, resigned and obedient.

He took out the chicken nuggets and placed them on a plate. He saw that they were too big for her to swallow all at once and so he cut them up and then poured the honey mustard sauce all over them, making sure each one got a fair amount. Placing the plate before her on the floor, he reminded her to keep her hands behind her back or he would have to tie them. She just nodded and complied.

He finished off his burger while she ate. She kept her hands clasped together behind the small of her back, spread her knees widely and then leaned her head over until she could slurp up individual pieces of the cut up chicken. It took her a while, so he had a smoke while he waited. He enjoyed watching her. He poured some of the Pepsi into a bowl and let her drink it. She would need the caffeine. When she was done, her wiped her face and cleaned the plate and bowl.

He showed her the denim miniskirts. She picked out the one that she thought would fit her best and, business like, stepped into it and snapped it closed. She looked much different with some clothes on. It made him want to fuck her. But they didn't have time. She picked out a light blue t-shirt with a bouquet of pink and yellow flowers on the front and put it on. He gave her the socks and the running shoes and they seemed to fit fine. He carefully folded the little yellow dress and put it and the matching shoes in one of the plastic bags from the army navy store.

He ordered her into the bathroom and brought her bulging, yellow purse with him. She opened it and carefully outlined her eyes, powdered her face, applied her bright red lipstick. When everything was ready and packed, he gave her her new parka to wear. She looked like a whole other person. He had no illusions that she wouldn't try and run away if she got the chance, but he was also satisfied that as long as she was in his presence, she would be docile and subservient. He felt good about that because he had lost all desire to harm her.

He pulled the Walther out of the pocket of his cargo pants and showed it to her. Her eyes widened and she stepped back.

"I just wanted you to know. We'll be driving all night. We may have to make some stops. If you fuck up, if you endanger me, I will fucking shoot you dead in an instant. I want you to know that without any doubt. I don't want to hurt you, but I'm never going back to stir. They'll have to kill me first and I will kill anyone that gets in my way. And that includes you. Do you understand?"

She nodded her head. She understood.

They went out to the car. She stood by while he put the things in the back seat. He made her get in the driver's side. He knelt there with the door open and tied her left leg to the bottom of the seat. He gave it about 18" of slack. It would be just one more impediment to her running away. He closed the driver's door, hustled around to the passenger seat, got in and closed the door. He handed her the keys. She started the engine up, put the car in gear and they were on their way once more.

CHAPTER FOUR

It was a little after 7:30 that they got started. Carly was in a daze. It was almost like all feelings had left her. Her fear was completely gone. Or, not gone really, just kind of absent. It was like hanging off of a precipice by a rope and you knew that as long as you had hold of it you were all right. But the moment your hand began to slip, and you knew that that moment was inevitable, you would be filled with agonizing fear. For now, she was okay. She could take a breather from fear. But she knew that it might erupt again at any moment. For now, she was lost in an eddying rush of fate. The man was her guide. Wherever he took her, she would go. She was just along for the ride.

She felt the rope on her left leg as she drove. She felt like telling him that he didn't need it now. She wouldn't run. What was the sense? She pictured herself getting ten or fifteen feet away from the car, hearing a loud, 'Bang!' and then feeling a hole being punched in her back and erupting through her chest. No, she didn't want to die that way. If he was going to kill her, she was going to make him, if she could, do it as a conscious, voluntary, depraved act, not as some visceral reaction to a perceived threat. Somehow, she would count it as a victory if he did it with a conscious, premeditated blow.

There was more traffic than when they started out last night. They came into a built up area almost right away.

Several times they stopped at red lights with cars sitting right next to them in the next lane. Carly could see the people. They were going about their lives as if nothing had happened. Didn't they know that the whole world had changed?

It was funny, it kind of made her see how shallow her life had been. She never paid any attention to the news. It was just stuff happening to other people. She rarely left her home town. Randy was kind and sweet to her, but he was, when you came down to it, Mr. Average, a safe choice. Her job was safe and unchallenging. She had given up any idea of going to college and being something else than a menial laborer. She never read any books anymore. She never went out and met new people. It was too bad she was learning so late how boring and predictable her life had become, now that her life was, for all practical purposes over.

For it was over. The man was going to kill her. She knew it. She didn't want to hasten it. She would do whatever he said in order to breathe as many breaths as possible between now and then, live as much as she could live. And if it meant being the man's sex slave, if it meant receiving the pleasures of the caresses of her own assassin, she would do it. If her life was meant to end, she intended to squeeze every ounce of pleasure out of it that she could.

The man said nothing. He smoked, ate some chips. Smoked some more. His body was relaxed, but his eyes were always at work, scanning the road for police (they had seen a couple), danger, scanning her for any sign of rebellion. He was poised for action. She knew that if she started to talk, unless it was absolutely necessary, his fist would flash out like it did last night and strike her arm again, causing her disabling pain. He was tightly wound all right. And she was going to have to drive with him for almost 12 hours straight.

She thought of the blow job that she had given him when she had been released from her devilish confinements. It had amazed even her. She had never done anything like that before. Her life had never been in real danger before either. And neither had she been ever tied up unmercifully like that and had a man stand over her contemplating whether she should live or die. The best explanation she had for her behavior was that she wanted the man to know that she was his to do with as he liked. She would not resist him. And she would devote herself to his pleasure for as long as he would let her. And that she was sorry. Sorry for having offended him. Sorry for not understanding her place in this new world.

And it had been exciting! The most exciting thing she had ever done! Her heart began to beat a little faster now, while she was thinking of it. Her pussy began to burn. In a little more than 11 hours, she would be naked in his bed again. He would tie her up and use her, plow her with his magical prick. She would come again and again and again. And barring unforeseen catastrophe, she intended to be there tonight and obtain the pleasure she had earned.

At a little before 9, they drove into a built up area. Jack saw the sign for the bridge over the Mississippi. He had traveled this way a few times, running meth up to Minneapolis, delivering girls to their new pimps waiting for them in St. Paul, or to the Salvadorans waiting to run them down to Denver or places beyond. They usually drugged the girls all up, moved them two or three at a time in small vans. They would be given a shot in the basement of the clubhouse where they were kept pending sale or disposition, and wake up in a cage in the back of some other van heading to their new home.

He made the girl drive past the entrance to the bridge. He looked around carefully. This was the danger point. This is where they would be waiting. He saw nothing. About ten blocks past the bridge, he made her turn around and go past it again, slower this time. Still nothing. Maybe they were waiting for him on the other side, he thought. He didn't want to drive by the bridge too often otherwise some cop who wasn't even thinking about him might become suspicious and decide to make an inquiry.

They stopped about ten blocks past the bridge, back the way they came. He had her pull into a shopping center parking lot and turn around. He took out the gun.

"We're going to cross that bridge," he told her. "I want you to listen to whatever I say like it was the voice of God talking to you. I want instantaneous obedience. If I say, 'Turn right!' then turn right. If I say, 'Turn left!' then you do that. If I say to hit it, then I want you to put the pedal to the floor. Remember, the life you will save will be your own. You're my hostage and if the cops get us stopped, I intend to shoot it out. Understand?"

The girl nodded back at him. He expected to see more fear in her face, but he saw, instead, what looked like excitement. Well, it would be exciting if the cops were waiting. He had the two extra clips for the Walther and the rest of the handguns from the army navy store fully loaded and an arm's length away. "There will be a hail of bullets," he thought to himself. That's how the papers would describe it. The boys back at the pen would read it and know that he had gone down with flying colors, resolute to the last. And they would read about the girl and imagine for themselves the fun he had had with her before they died in a 'hail' of bullets. And they would be right. Fuckin' eh! And, hopefully, more to follow tomorrow.

He had her pull up to the bridge. It was a left hand turn off lane. The light for the turn was red. Her blinker was on. He had the Walther in his lap. He kept flicking the safety on and off. He had already chambered a bullet. The light turned green. She looked quickly over at him, as if for permission, and then she edged the car across the opposite lane of traffic and entered the bridge lane. They went up a small ramp and then, presto, they were on the bridge.

The Mississippi here is not the thunderous river that it is down by Missouri and the more southern states. But it's big enough. The water runs fast and strong. It has already been gaining momentum for over 250 miles. The bridge was steel frame with two lanes in each direction. It was relatively crowded for its 500 foot length and brightly lit. Jack was keeping his eyes peeled for any untoward movement on the other side or, for that matter, behind him. It would be a great place to trap him, with cops on both sides and just the river below.

But nothing happened. The light was green on the other side. They sailed right through it. "Turn left," he told he girl. They headed south.

He leaned back and reached for a smoke, keeping half an eye on the rearview mirror. He lit it and looked at the girl. She seemed to have a sense of relaxation on her face too. It would have been a wild shoot out, that's for sure. Her chances of survival would have been from slim to none. Apparently she knew it and that she had dodged a bullet, so to speak. She had done a good job, was cool from beginning to end. She had balls. He liked that.

The area was fairly well built up and the road was somewhat congested. Traffic was traveling at a decent pace though and soon they were out of the urbanized area near the bridge.

Just on the outskirts of the town, Jack saw something that intrigued him. It was an adult movie, book and novelty store. It was called the Whip and Chain. The front window was painted over to conceal the nature of the merchandise and to cloak the customers in anonymity. He ordered the girl to pull into the parking lot.

It was a brown, wooden, one story structure. The back of the store fronted the road and all the parking was away from the street, something that suited Jack. He ordered the girl to pull into a parking space. There was only one other car there which Jack assumed was for the store clerk. It was a little after 9:30 and the sign on the tinted, glass door said that the store closed at 10. Before going into the store, Jack reminded the girl of the pistol in his pocket and the necessity of absolute obedience.

They walked in.

The store was small, about 30' by 30'. The clerk sat behind a long, Formica counter. In front were several dozen garish and salacious publications. Behind the clerk, on the wall, were thirty or so different x-rated DVDs with voluptuous, willing, inviting, naked women on the covers. The clerk was dressed in a rust red t-shirt with the name of the store on it, a denim vest and blue jeans. He was balding, about 35 or so, and wore a scraggly beard. His shoulders were broad and he stood maybe 6'2". His middle bulged. There was an earring in his left ear made of gold. His forearms carried tattoos of strange, Asiatic style designs. He was reading a magazine. He barely looked at them.

Jack pulled the girl down one of the aisles. There were various sex aids: dildos, ticklers, masturbation aids, a blow up doll and more. Picking up a basket, Jack advanced to the aisle proffering bondage and discipline goods. He saw what he wanted right away. It was a six inch long, thick black prong connected to a leather belt. He picked a package off the shelf. Next, he selected a leather gag with straps that went around the back of the head. This too had a prong. Jutting out of the inside was a five inch long, rubbery, yet firm, model of a circumcised penis. He put it in the basket. Next, he selected four black leather bracelets with soft, fuzzy interiors and rings on the outside and a matching collar. He selected two sets of chains, one 18" long and the other about 6". Finally, he picked out a bag of small locks that all worked off of the same key.

He dragged her by the arm back to the checkout counter. The clerk processed the items nonchalantly, barely looking up at them. Jack paid cash.

Carly was shocked at the man's selections, knowing full well they were intended for her body. She wanted desperately to run outside the store, but knew that she would probably not even make it to the door. Once the man paid, "With my fucking money!" she thought, she made ready to go back out to the car. He grabbed her arm and held her back. He pushed her so that she was about a foot away from the counter. "Bend over," he ordered.

Carly suppressed a sob. She knew he was going to do something she wouldn't like, something humiliating and degrading. She looked at the sales clerk whose interest had been captured by the man's sharp command.

The man saw her hesitation. "I said bend over," he repeated gruffly, a fierce determination on his face. "Or do you want me to get one of the whips they have on display here?"

She saw that he meant business. She knew that she had three choices. She could resist and get beaten, and then probably do what he wanted anyway, or run and get a bullet between her shoulder blades. Or, her third choice, she could just comply. The store clerk was looking at her like he was anticipating a show and clearly had no sympathy for her predicament. Of course, he did not know the full extent of it, but he knew that she had been offered a stark choice. He would probably enjoy seeing her whipped. Maybe he would even close the store so that the man could really lay into her, do a complete job.

She laid her torso across the counter. The clerk's face was only a foot or so away from hers. Her lips were trembling, her hands were balled up into little fists. She heard the man opening the packaging. He placed the torn cardboard and shrink wrap on the counter. There was a pause and then she saw him place the tube of lubricant on the counter next to it. She realized that he had had it in his pocket.

There was a moment of agonizing silence. She imagined him spreading the lubricant over the thick, black, plastic prong. She looked up at the clerk. He was smiling sardonically. The man behind her spoke.

"Back up and spread your legs," he told her. She obeyed. His hands reached under her short, denim skirt and lifted it, exposing her naked rear end. She felt him place the leather belt around her waist and buckle it tightly against her bare skin. The prong and a pair of thin chains dangled down over her buttocks. He spread her rear cheeks apart. She closed her eyes and whined her dismay. She felt the thick head of the device beg entrance.

It came up against her delicate rear ring, spread it apart and then, aided by the lubricant, began to slide in.

A feeling of sickness spread through her body as she felt the object enter her most private place. She moaned as her anal ring stretched to accommodate it and whined as it filled her. It hurt. Not as much as it did when he had fucked her there earlier. But what was worse than the hurt was the humiliation of having it inside her, stretching her, she knew, so that when he used her tomorrow, wherever it was that they stopped, he would be able to enter her with ease.

His hands wrapped back around her waist and then dipped down between her legs, capturing the little chains that ran from the base of the object now fully lodged inside her. He aligned them along the sides of her hairless love lips and then brought them up to the belt around her waist. She felt him run them through an eyelet there, pulling them tight, and forcing the object in her rectum deeper inside her. He then affixed them in place.

Jack marveled at the wonderful sight of the girl prostrate before him, her delicate thighs spread, the anal plug peeping from her rear. He rubbed her buttocks. His cock was rock hard and he felt like fucking her right there. He reached between her legs and stroked her pussy. She was wet. He laughed to himself. He knew she didn't like it. How could she like it? But it made her hot all the same. He stroked and played with her pussy while the store clerked looked on. He knew that she was desperate to call out to him for help. It was ironic that he was so eagerly viewing her, would probably remember her for a long, long time, but probably never know her true status as an abject prisoner whose very life stood on a razor's edge.

The girl's knees sagged and she moaned. The clerk laughed.

"She's hot all right," he said. "How much to fuck her?"

It was Jack's turn to laugh. "I don't know. I hadn't really thought about it. I could probably use a few bucks. What do you think she's worth?"

He took hold of her hair and pulled her body away from the counter. "Lift your skirt," he told her.

The girl whined, but she did what she was told. She took her miniskirt in her hands and lifted the front until it was up around her waist. Her pretty, hairless pussy, with the two brass chains on either sides of it, was displayed in all its glory. She went to bring her legs together, but thought twice of it. "Smart cookie," Jack thought.

"How's about 50 bucks?" the man asked.

"Bullshit!" Jack answered him. "She's worth more then that! How about $500? She's new on the game, almost a cherry."

"Whoa, man," the clerk replied. "That's way outta my league. Anyways, no pussy's worth 500 bucks. How much for just a blow job?"

"I don't think she's for sale tonight," Jack said. He had circled his hand between her legs and was playing with her pussy again. "But I tell you what. I'll bring her around again in a few weeks after I've had her on the game a bit and I'll bring the price down. How's that?"

"I'll be right here," the clerk answered.

The man unwrapped the penis gag and turned back to Carly. "Open your mouth," he told her. Lips trembling, her pussy still exposed, her dress hiked up to her waist, tears flowing down her face, she obeyed. She watched as he brought the offensive object to her mouth. It looked just like a stiffened, if truncated cock. It passed over her lips and entered her mouth, pushing her tongue down and filling her oral cavity. The man went behind her and connected the belt behind her head tightly, forcing the penis like probe all the way to the back near her throat. Her mouth clamped around it. The leather guard to which it was attached covered her forcibly spread apart lips and curled under her chin, forcing her jaw upwards and closing her mouth around the offensive presence. It made her think of his cock in her mouth earlier today. And, of course, that was the point. It had been between her lips and would be again. The gag was just a placeholder for it, one that would remind her implacably, as if she really needed it, of her utter subservience to him.

He fastened the collar around her neck and attached the bracelets to her ankles and wrists. He was going to attach one of the steel chains he had purchased to the brass ring in the front of her collar, but the clerk stopped him.

"Here," he said, handing Jack a five foot long leash with a shiny red leather handle. "It's on the house."

Jack thanked him and clipped its end to the girl's collar.

"And here," the clerk added. "Take this too. It works really good."

He handed Jack a package containing an egg shaped object and what looked like a TV remote. Jack looked at it.

"You put it in her pussy," the clerk told him. "The zapper turns it on and off. It vibrates inside and drives them wild. It's got a high, low and medium. Put it on high and I guarantee you, she'll come all over her seat."

Jack smiled. He tore the package apart and put some lube over the egg like object. "Here," he said to the clerk, "you put it in."

A grin spread over the clerk's face. He quickly came around the counter and took the egg from Jack's hand. Carly winced with shame as he approached her. Her hands, which were still obediently holding up her blue, denim miniskirt, started to tremble. She tried to utter a word of protest, but it just got muffled by the fiendish gag.

"Spread you legs some more, honey," the clerk told her. He towered over her. Between the two men, she felt like she was a tiny, alien creature that they had captured. She looked at the man she had come to know as Blackjack Jackson, the conscienceless killer, in the hopes of urging him to mercy, but he just looked at her sternly. She spread her legs.

The clerk approached her closely. She closed her eyes. Despite her shame, despite her revulsion at what was happening to her, she was unhappily aroused and she knew that the clerk would find her pussy wet and receptive. She could feel the heat of his body. His hand went down between her legs and she felt the egg press up against her labia. It was cool and hard. He pressed it forward. It was larger than her tunnel was at rest and it swelled her innards as it passed her love lips and entered her. The clerk's rough hand lingered on the outside of her sex, rubbing itself up and down several times and teasing her hardened clit. Then he stepped away.

"Turn it on," he told Jack.

Jack fingered the control and pressed a button. A faint hum emerged from the girl's pussy. Her eyes widened and her hips dipped as if she had fallen into a swoon. She looked at him anxiously. He smiled at her and turned it up. She winced as the humming got louder. Her eyebrows formed a frown and she started to lower her hands so as to cover herself. A whine escaped from behind her gag.

"Put your hands back up," Jack spat out at her.

She complied unhappily. She desperately wanted to bring her knees together to try and fight off the lust driving sensations that were emerging from the egg. Her eyes flitted back and forth between the clerk and her captor. "Please stop it! Please!' she thought. And then she saw Jack's finger move again on the control. The vibrations accelerated instantly sending a wave of feverish lust through her. "Mmmmmmmmmmmmmmm!" she moaned unhappily. 'Ummmmmmmmmmmmmmmm!" Her heart was thumping in her chest and her body had broken out in sweat. Her knees felt weak and she felt dizzy.

And then, she couldn't help it. Her knees gave out and she fell to the floor. She bent over and squeezed her legs together. Her hands balled into little fists. Her whole body shuddered. Her pussy erupted into a volcanic explosion. It throbbed and convulsed and spasmed. It felt like it had come alive between her thighs. She jammed her eyes shut and her teeth sank into the intruder in her mouth. She moaned, long and loud.

Then, just as fast as it started, the egg's vibrations ceased. Her pussy's eruptions slowed and her body relaxed. She started to cry. The man's control over her was insidious, devilish. "What's happening to me?" she asked herself miserably.

Jack and the clerk laughed. "Thanks, bud," Jack said. He pulled on the chain attached to the girl's collar. "Get up, cunt," he told her. She looked up at him dolefully and then rose from her knees.

"See you in a couple of weeks," Jack told he clerk. Then he led his prisoner from the store. He knew for sure he would never see the man again.

After that, they drove for three hours straight almost due south. He had fastened Carly's left ankle to the underside of the driver's seat using the long chain he had bought. With the short chain, he connected her wrists, running it through the steering wheel so that her hands were locked in place. Carly's emotions ran from fear and hatred of her captor to a woeful self pity for her situation. She could not ignore the foreign objects that were penetrating her, or forget that as soon as they stopped somewhere, they would be replaced by the real thing. It was horrible to have the faux cock in her mouth. Every time her mouth squeezed it when she swallowed it made her feel sick. Her own weight pressed the prong in her rear deeply inside her. It made her bowel feel so full and open. A couple times, the man started the egg vibrating in her pussy and her lusts would build up until she trembled and moaned. Then he would shut it off, chuckling to himself.

A little after 1 a.m. they stopped at a Burger King. Before they pulled up to the drive up window, the man removed her gag and released her hands from the steering wheel. He ordered a Coke and a Whopper for himself and some more chicken nuggets and a bottle of water for her, which he hand fed to her. After they ate, he pulled to a dark part of the parking lot and let her pee on the tarmac. He peed too and then they were off again.

He wanted to make at least 500 miles tonight. He had the girl keep off the Interstate and main highways and stay along the back roads. It was time consuming and the roads were dark. Once into Iowa, the roads became straight and true and they did a little better. He had her change direction often, varying between heading due south and westerly. That way, he hoped, he stayed off any predictable path.

Around 4:30 they crossed the Nebraska border and reached the outskirts of Omaha. He had the gag off the girl a few more times when they stopped for gas and peed again. He could see that she was dragging ass. She hadn't got a lot of sleep the day before and her evening had been a lot more stressful than his. When he saw her nodding off, he had her pull off the road. He would drive.

He turned off the engine and came around to the driver's side. The night was pitch black and there were no streetlights anywhere near them. The road was a long straightaway so he could see any cars coming in either direction a long time before they arrived. He unlocked her foot from under the seat and had her get out of the car. She was practically asleep on her feet.

He turned her around and drew her arms behind her, locking her wrist bracelets together. She had not put her dark blue parka on that he had provided for her and so she was dressed just in her t-shirt and denim miniskirt. Seizing her by the arm, he took her to the back of the car. He used the key fob to pop the trunk.

The girl's eyes widened. "…..eeeeeeeeease! ….on't!" she moaned from behind her gag. He paid no attention to her and pushed her in. He fastened her ankle bracelets together and connected them to her bound wrists. She was crying and she gave him a desperate, forlorn look just as he slammed the trunk lid shut.

He would drive now. She could rest or not as she chose. He couldn't have her sit in the passenger seat because he wouldn't be able to keep an eye on her and the road at the same time. The same thing went for the back seat. That left the trunk. It was a no brainer.

He got into the driver's side, revved up the engine and got back on the road.

He smoked, drank from the Pepsi bottle and relaxed, gazing out at his own headlamps as they pierced the dark night before him, guiding his way to freedom. He felt energized. It was too bad the girl had to be in the trunk. He liked looking at her thighs, her unhappy, gagged face, her full breasts, while she drove. But it couldn't be helped. And, besides, it was nice to have the car to himself for a while.

He turned on the radio. He had to hit a few buttons until he got a decent station. There was about another hour of darkness left. He would need to start looking for a place for them to stay. He wanted to find one with cabins like the last one. That had been ideal. And it was more likely that he would find one away from a city. The next big one coming up was Kansas City. Just thinking the words brought the old song back to him.

> "I'm going to Kansas City.
> Kansas City here I come
> Oh, I'm going to Kansas City.
> Kansas City here I come.
> They've got some crazy little women there,
> And I'm going to get me one."

He laughed and pushed down on the pedal, revving up the speed just a notch.

Carly had drifted off to sleep. The man had been right. She had been exhausted. At first, she had been terrified to be locked in the trunk of her own car. A thousand different pictures, none of them good, sprung into her mind. She twisted and turned her bound limbs to no avail and sobbed and sobbed. For more than 24 hours now, she had not made one volitional movement. Everything had been imposed on her. The objects that the man had placed in and on her body were part of that. Even the clothes she was wearing now. She was a totally controlled human being. And what frightened her was how easily he was able to generate lust in her. The scene at the adult toy store had been a case in point. Once he lifted her skirt in the presence of the store clerk, she had been off to the races. A terrible lust had flowed through her body when the man made her show the clerk her bare, naked pussy. When the egg had been placed inside her by that strange man, her pussy turned feverish. It was no wonder that all the man had to do was turn the egg to vibrate to get her to moan and cream in front of them.

She tried to shift her uncomfortable body, wishing that she had put her parka on before she got out of the car. She realized that the trunk was a lot more crowded than she usually kept it and she wondered what the man had acquired while he had been away from the little cabin. She moved her head and the presence of the prick like intruder in her mouth came home to her. It was like the worse nightmare she had ever had. She was a prisoner of a madman and he kept doing worse and worse things to her. She had no chance of escape, not even the slightest hope. And all that she could see in her future was doom. Doom as black as the dark space around her.

When she awoke, she heard the radio on. It was very cold. The image of him sitting comfortably in her front seat, smoking those stinky cigarettes and fiddling with the radio angered her. It was so unfair. Everything that had happened was so unfair. She pulled and tugged at her bonds and tried to emit a roar of rage from behind her gag. All that emerged was a mere murmur.

And then she heard it. The news was on. She had missed the first few words. And then her hearing just zoned in on it as if the man inside the car had turned the radio up.

> "...Wisconsin authorities believe that Jackson kidnapped 22 year old Carly Walker just outside of the small town of Beaver Dam yesterday evening at about 11 P.M. They are concentrating their search for the escaped murderer and his prisoner in the Wausau area where Jackson once led a notorious chapter of the outlaw motorcycle gang, the Rouges. He is believed to be driving Ms. Walker's maroon, 1996 Chevrolet Malibu and to be armed and dangerous. His photograph and that of Ms. Walker are available on the Wisconsin Attorney General's website. Federal authorities, we are told, have focused their search for Jackson in areas west and south of Wisconsin in the belief that he may have fled the state......In other news....."

The radio clicked off.

Jack sat back and grimaced. Well, the jig was up with the girl. He knew it couldn't last forever. Anyone who saw her and the car together in one place would add two and two and make four. One of them had to go. And right now, he only had one car.

At least he knew that his ruse at throwing the authorities off his trail had worked. The main area of search for him was concentrated in his old stomping grounds. That's why it was so easy to get across the Mississippi back there.

But then there was that thing about the FBI. They knew where he was headed. It would probably have taken them a day or so to get a real operation going, but they were probably hot on his trail now. It wouldn't take them long to connect the job at the army navy store with him and from there calculate how far west or south he could have gone. All the Interstates and main highways would be watched closely.

He was about fifteen miles outside of Kansas City. The area was heavily wooded with nice rolling hills. He had to do something right away. He had to get rid of the car. But first he had to get rid of his excess baggage.

About a mile down the road, he took a turnoff to the west. He drove for about twenty minutes. The terrain was getting flatter but more heavily wooded. Finally, he saw what he was looking for. It was an old dirt road. He turned into it. It went on for about 3 or 4 miles. He passed one run down old house, but nothing else. Another, even narrower road, one even less traveled on, went off to the left. He took it. Abut a mile up there was a small clearing. He pulled the car into it and shut off the engine.

A deep pit had been growing in Carly's belly. She knew that whoever had connected her kidnapping to the man's escape and announced it to the world had signed her death warrant. He had to get rid of her now. Her picture would be all over the news. They would have a description if not a picture of her car. No way could they walk together into a motel lobby now. The law would be there fifteen minutes after they checked in. No, he would travel alone from here on out.

A dismal fatalism ran through her. She had been expecting it all along and here it was. She closed her eyes and tried to pray.

The roughness of the ride and their reduction in speed told her that they had pulled down some old dirt road somewhere. He was taking her some place remote where he could kill her and leave her body. When the car stopped, she knew that she had only minutes to live.

The trunk popped open within a few moments. He released her ankles from her wrists and lifted her body out of the trunk. She was unsteady on her feet and he had to hold her up by her arm for a little while so she wouldn't fall. His grip was like iron. Carly knew that escape from him was impossible.

She tried not to look him in the face. She didn't want his cruelty to be the last thing that she saw. When he told her to start walking into the woods, she didn't refuse. What was the point? She wanted to maintain her dignity as long as she could.

But she couldn't stop the crying. She thought of Randy and the life they thought they had together. Of her mother who she had never made up with after their foolish argument. Of the girls she worked with, of Ike, her girlhood friends, her past boyfriends. It all came rushing through her mind.

After about a hundred yards he made her stop. This is as good a place as any, she thought. She looked up toward the trees. The morning light made everything seem dream like. She took a deep breath, enjoying the taste of the air. She hated the idea that they would find her body with all these things in it, but there was nothing she could do about it. There was nothing she could do about anything.

He pulled the Walther out of his pants pocket. The girl was looking away from him. He could hear her crying. She was tough though, he thought. No begging or pleading, no protest at all. It was too bad. And he had really been looking forward to fucking her again. He drew back the action and loaded a bullet into the chamber. It made a clicking sound that caused the girl to jump a little. He extended his arm. He wanted it to be a clean shot. Sudden death. It was the least he could do. He took a deep breath.

He waited. And waited. And waited. His hand started to shake. Something came boiling up inside him. "God damn it! Shoot!" he yelled to himself. "Shoot!"

He couldn't do it. It was useless to try. He lowered his gun hand.

His heart was beating a mile a minute. He was all sweaty and a little dizzy. Why couldn't he shoot her, he wondered. And then he knew it. There was something about the girl that he really liked. He just wasn't depraved enough to snuff it out. All those long years in stir he had thought about that girl that Drummer had made him kill. He knew that killing this girl now would haunt him just as much. More.

The guards he had killed and that guy at the army navy store, well, he didn't feel so bad about those. They were necessary. But this wasn't really necessary. It was just convenient. He could hide her in the trunk or leave her out here in the woods all tied up and maybe call in a couple of days and let the cops know where she was. But either way would cause problems. She might get away or something and then where would he be? His only hope was to have the FBI looking for him over thousands and thousands of miles. He hated his indecision.

Her whole body had been shaking as she had antici-pated the noise of the gun. She realized that she probably wouldn't even hear it. The bullet would snuff out her consciousness too fast. It would be just like turning out a light. But waiting for it was agonizing. "Just do it! Do it!" she screamed inside her.

And then he told her to get on her knees. "I should refuse," she thought. "I'd rather die on my feet." But then the thought that she might live just a few moments more if she obeyed him changed her mind. She sank down, one knee at a time and then knelt up straight.

"On your belly," he told her.

She turned to look at him. What was he up to? Why didn't he just shoot her? She saw the gun dangling from his right hand. It didn't look like he was going to use it. Had he changed his mind? "Oh god!" Carly thought. Her tears turned into sobs. He came close to her and, pushed her until she was face down on the ground. She felt him hook her ankles back together and then connect them again to her wrists.

Jack ejected the shell from the chamber of the Walther, making sure he retrieved it, and then put the pistol back in his pocket. There were things that he had to do. First thing he had to set things up so that he could leave her here while he went and got a new car. It might take most of the day so he had to be sure she was secure.

He went back to the car and got the camping stuff out of the trunk. He brought the tent over to where the girl was laying. First he dug out a depression using the little shovel that came with the camping kit, four feet long and about 6 or 8 inches deep. Then he set up the two man tent right over it. The tent was made of green and brown camouflage so it would be hard to spot.

Once the tent was up, he went back to the girl and unfastened her ankles. He pulled her to her feet and guided her to the tent. Before putting her in, he let her pee. Then he forced her in and made her lie down in the depression he had made. He hogtied her again using the bracelets. He knew that that wasn't enough. Somehow she might slip the bracelets over her ankles or wrists. He went outside the tent and got the rope he had used on her yesterday. He used it to tie off her elbows and knees, just like when she was in the tub. She squealed unhappily when her elbows came together. Then he tied off her wrists and ankles again as a second line of defense. If she was able to somehow to remove the bracelets, she would still have to get the ropes off.

When she was secure, although moaning unhappily, he stepped out of the tent. He walked back to the car and retrieved all their goods and piled them in the tent with the girl. He began removing all of the poles, making the top of the tent fall down on top of her. He straightened the stretch nylon as much as he could. He gathered some rocks and placed them at the corners so that the wind would not blow the top around. Then, after dragging some large branches over, he collected armfuls of dead leaves and brush and spread them out all over it. It was good and camouflaged. You would have to walk right up almost on top of it to see it, and maybe not even then. The girl would stay right where she was for as long as he wanted.

He stepped over to the edge of the tent and crouched down. "I have to go get another car," he told her. "I'll be back in a while. Stay right where you are. If I find out you've moved when I come back, I'll punish you."

He got up, surveyed his handiwork, and then walked back to the car.

CHAPTER FIVE

Agent Holmes and his young assistant were sitting in a coffee shop in the Treadway Motel in Iowa City, Iowa. He was not a happy man. That son of a bitch, publicity hound attorney general up in Wisconsin had blown the whole thing. Holmes had his men spread out over four states, Nebraska, Iowa, Kansas and Missouri. He had alerted the state police in each jurisdiction. Everybody was looking for a maroon Malibu and a blond headed girl. Now, because of that stupid asshole back in Wisconsin, they would have to start all over at square one. Their man would ditch the car and the girl and finding him would be like finding a needle in a haystack.

He had already instructed his people to double check every stolen car report in the target states. Any one of them could be Jackson, especially the older ones with antitheft systems that he was familiar with. They were going through all the other crime reports too. There had been one this morning in western Wisconsin that had piqued his interest. A store clerk had been killed in an army navy store outside of Tucker Lake. His throat had been slit ear to ear. All the money in the safe was missing and all the handguns in the display case.

Jackson's signature was all over the job. They were waiting for confirmation of some prints that they found, but they found probably a hundred sets in the public portion of the store. It would take a while to sift through them. But Holmes knew his man and was convinced that he had done it. It confirmed his hunch that he had headed west and crossed over the Mississippi last night. They had drawn on a map the outward limits of where they thought he could be by driving all night on back roads and they had decided that the furthest he could have gone was described by an arc that stretched from Denver, through Wichita and to St. Louis.

Things were complicated now that their man was certainly armed. And he had undoubtedly changed clothes and gotten a change of clothes for the girl, that is, if he hadn't killed her already. Holmes had seen Jackson's psychological profile and criminal history from the prison. He was smart all right. And he was as cold as cash. He had run half the prison and was notorious for striking back at any challenge to his authority. It was suspected that even a guard had fallen afoul of him. They had found his body at the bottom of some concrete stairs. The investigation concluded that he had fallen. The minority view was that he had been murdered.

And from his days out on the street, Holmes learned that Jackson had a thing for the ladies. The gang had run them sure enough, and he had a habit of picking out the cream of the crop for his own bed, using them and then throwing them away. Holmes was convinced that Jackson would keep the girl as long as he could. He wouldn't be able to resist it, especially after all that time behind the wall. The girl was good looking and young and that didn't hurt her chances at all. Until now, that is. Now her negatives would outweigh her positives.

He looked at his assistant, Special Agent Linda Kramer. She was bright and good looking and bucking for promotion. Blond and blue eyed, tall and lean. He had a job for her. She would be flying out later this morning. It was dangerous, but he had a hunch and wanted to play it out.

"Okay, Agent Kramer," he said, "here's what I want you to do…."

* * * * * * * * * * * * * * *

Jack took another cruise round the long term parking lot at the Kansas City International Airport. He didn't want to keep driving around and around, but he was looking for something special. He had picked up the tools he needed at a local hardware store.

He saw a metallic blue, '94 Mercury Grand Marquee pull into the lot and pass him. It looked perfect. Jack circled around and parked the Malibu. He got out and nonchalantly walked over to where the Marquee was parking. A guy wearing a somewhat shabby, ill fitting business suit got out. He popped the trunk and removed a valise, a small, wheeled suitcase and a large garment bag. It looked like the guy was going for a long trip.

Once the man exited the lot to head towards the terminal, Jack went to work. He quickly jimmied open the door with the flat bar he stuck in by the driver's side window. It took him a couple of tries to catch the mechanism just right, but then the door unlocked and popped open. Casting a quick look around, Jack then hopped in the car. He had the ignition lock off in about ten seconds. The screwdriver went into the ignition, he turned it and the engine leapt into life. He looked down at the dashboard. There was ¾ of a tank of gas. The inside of the car was as clean as a whistle just like the guy had tidied it up knowing that someone else was going to use it. Jack didn't wait to examine the rest of the car. He put it in reverse, backed it out slowly from its slot and then headed for the gate. He had the ticket from the Malibu. He drove up to the ticket window. When the guy in the booth looked at the ticket, he looked back quickly at Jack.

"Changed my mind," Jack told him. He handed him a twenty. The guy handed him back his change with a sneer. Jack pulled off.

He made a few stops on his way back to where he had left the girl. He stocked up on some food and sundries at this huge grocery store, bigger than any he had ever been in. They had just about everything he needed there. He stopped to top off the gas tank. In the convenience store next to the gas station, he saw something in the window that intrigued him. It was an advertisement for a cell phone for $50.00. He went into the shop. He discovered that he didn't have to show any identification to get one. He made up a name and bought one. It would come in handy later, he was sure.

Before going to pick up the girl, he pulled the car to a remote location and inspected it. It had 137,000 miles. There were maps and other paperwork in the glove box, including the registration. The car belonged to a Peter Lindley. Why people kept their registration in their glove box was beyond him. The ash tray was full of change. There was a picture of a woman under the visor on the driver's side. She was a pretty brunette, likely Lindley's girlfriend or wife.

In the trunk was nothing remarkable aside from a spare tire, some tools and a case of bottled water.

A little while later, Jack pulled up to the dirt road he had gone down earlier where he had left the girl. He slowed down, but just kept going. He had been away a little more than 4 hours. What if the girl had gotten loose and had got in contact with the cops? They could be waiting for him there. It was stupid to drive down a single lane road when there might be someone waiting to slaughter him. He drove on for about 2 miles and then turned around. It was a little before noon. He needed to put some distance between himself and the airport as soon as possible. There was always the possibility that the guy had gone back to his car for some reason. Maybe his flight was cancelled, or maybe he forgot something and had to go back to the car to get it, one of the many indecipherable papers in the glove box. The whole point of changing cars was so that the Feds wouldn't know what he was driving. Why take time to get the girl? He had food. He had money. And he had the Walther and its extra clips. He could just leave the stuff he had unloaded from the girl's car. He didn't really need it.

But if he didn't get the girl, the likelihood was that she would die out there all tied up like that. It was getting colder and the radio had said that there was a cold front coming in with the probability of snow. At least a foot, they said. The girl would probably freeze to death overnight. It was probably below freezing already. He knew that the girl's death would linger on his conscience no matter whether she died from a bullet he put into the back of her head, or died because he left her tied up in the woods in the middle of a blizzard. The only difference was that he wouldn't have to see her die.

He was parked in the lot of a convenience store. He knew that he needed to get on his way before somebody got suspicious. But what should he do? He slammed his hand into the steering wheel. "Fuck!" he yelled. He knew he needed sleep. He had been up close to 24 hours. And he needed to make tracks. But it sure would be nice to have the girl with him when he stopped to get some. He thought of her mouth around his cock, the way she had sucked him off before they had left the cabin yesterday. And her ass would be nice and stretched, easy to get into. She had sweet tits and she kissed him back fiercely when he got her excited.

His cock had grown hard just thinking about her. "Fuck!" he repeated, not quite so loudly this time. He knew he was going to go get her. He was just stalling for time. He didn't want to face what might be down that road. He was so close to getting away. It would be a shame to die now. He took a deep breath. "Okay, let's do it," he thought. He put the car back into gear and drove back to the little dirt road.

Once he entered it, he kept the Walther on his lap. He had the two extra clips in his pocket. There was no way they would take him alive.

The car edged its way slowly down the road. His eyes were peeled for any sign of movement. He went a little further. Nothing. When the car came to the cutoff, he took it, the driver's window open and the gun in his hand. He pulled up to where the Malibu had been parked. He saw the tire tracks. He looked around. The sky had turned grey and there were a few flakes of snow coming down. The place looked desolate.

He walked the 100 yards or so to where he had buried the girl under the brush. He stopped. If he listened very close, he could hear a sound like whimpering, although it might just have been the wind through the leafless trees. He looked down at the pile of desiccated leaves and branches. Maybe she was dead already, he thought. He didn't want to dig her out if she was. He would rather remember her alive. He lit a smoke. He gave it some thought. Finally, he decided that he might as well get his stuff as long as he was here anyways. If she was dead, then, maybe it was fate and not him who killed her. Maybe it was just her time to go.

He tossed aside the smoke and began to drag off the debris he had used to cover the tent. As he progressed, the whimpering sound became louder. Once the brush was clear, he pulled off the top of the tent. There she was, squirming and squealing.

It had been awful. At first, Carly had struggled with her bonds uselessly. Then she realized that with the stuff all piled on top of her, she had limited air. If she used it all up, she might suffocate. She tried to calm herself. He said he would be back in a while. What's a while? An hour? Two? He can't mean longer than that. That would be horrible. As it was it was horrible, but it would be so much worse if she had to wait that long for liberation.

After a short time, she relaxed. "I should just be glad I'm alive," she thought. When she had heard the click of the pistol, she thought it was all over. All of her senses had gathered together in unity to live that final moment. Her mind had never been so concentrated in all of her life. She had never been so alert to her individuality in the world, her separateness from it. The world would continue and she would not. It would go on for months and years and decades and centuries. Her body would wither and decay. Eventually, even her bones would turn to dust. Her presence would be extinguished. Everyone she knew would mourn her and she would not be able to say a single thing to them.

Her life had been leading inexorably to this single moment and she had never suspected it. In a split second she would have the answer to the age old questions. Would she see God? Would she see her father who had gone on before her? Would she see paradise? Or would all consciousness merely black out into nothingness? Would it hurt?

All these things went rushing away when the man told her to get on her knees. She had started to sob uncontrollably. Somehow her nerves had been shattered by that single command. But when he pushed her to her belly and started binding her legs together, she realized that he had changed his mind. Again. Twice now she had been brought to the edge of annihilation and had survived.

The dam broke. She cried and cried and cried. She heard the man moving around and doing something, but she didn't have the energy to care. All she knew was that she was still breathing, still feeling, still thinking. When she heard him digging, she got nervous again, but then she looked up and saw him setting up the tent. Were they going to stay in it? It would be cold and uncomfortable. But she didn't care. She would stay anywhere.

Then the man led her over, and made her lie down inside the tent. Due to the hole he had made, her shoulders and belly were about six inches below the level of the surrounding ground. He tied her elbows together just like yesterday and then hooked her legs back up to her wrists. He tied them too. And her knees. He was making doubly sure that she wouldn't get away. She realized that she owed her life to the value he saw in her.

She thought back to that blowjob she had given him just before they left the cabin last night. She hadn't really known what she was doing at the time. She had just reacted to an urge, a need to prove her worth to him. Now she realized that that blowjob had probably saved her life. As long as she was willing and open and a valuable sexual object, he would want her and let her live. It was a lesson she would remember.

He brought all their stuff into the tent and then lowered it over her. She heard and felt him covering her with something, leaves and branches. Then she heard his voice. He would be back.

She kept going back to that promise as the time dragged on. He said he would be back. But as the time got longer and longer, doubt began to creep into her mind. She couldn't see anything. The dark nylon of the tent admitted almost no light. It was getting cold, freezing cold, and her muscles were way past cramping. She was hungry. She was frightened. Maybe he changed his mind. Maybe he got arrested and decided not to tell them where she was. Maybe he had an accident. Or maybe he shot it out with the cops and he's dead and them with no clue as to what he did with her. She had no idea where she was. All she knew was that she was in some woods somewhere. They had driven a long time on that bumpy road when she was in the trunk. She could be miles from the nearest house.

The longer she lay there, the more frightened she got. She would vary from certitude that he was never coming back to a firm resolution that all she had to do was to hang on to her sanity and everything would be all right. He had promised. But then, he was a convict, a murderer. What good was a promise from him? And then she would start all over again.

She realized that he had gone to steal another car. She wondered how long that would take him. He had to go to some urbanized setting so that the car wouldn't be missed right away. She had no idea how far away from one they were. She tried to visualize a map in her head. They had gone west the night before last and then south and west and south and west last night. She knew that they had crossed into Nebraska at some point before he put her in the trunk, but that was all she knew.

From time to time, she struggled at her bonds. She knew it was useless, but she couldn't help herself. She tried not to do it because each time that she stopped, the realization that it was useless would produce a wave of intense misery that would flow all through her. It was so hard to accept what had been happening to her. It was so hard to accept in her mind that she couldn't move her hands or legs, that she was completely helpless, lying in a hole somewhere out in the wilderness, unable to move more than a smidgeon of an inch in any direction. It was so hard to accept that the only person in the whole world who was likely to save her from her current horrid circumstances was the man who put her here.

She thought about the knots that held her so tightly bound. They were a product of the man's will. It made it seem like he could project it on her from wherever he went, whatever he did. The knots were like stored up energy, a force produced by his steely muscles, his iron like grip, and transferred to the rope that bound her. It was almost like an act of magic, like she was being held in place by some evil spell he had placed upon her. Her mouth was still stuffed with that foul gag. That thing was still in her rear and that egg thing in her sex. He had placed them there and there they would remain until he removed them. He had buried her in the wilderness, worked his charms on her and then left her here to molt like some weird chrysalis.

Would she emerge as a butterfly? Something beautiful and magical? Or maybe, she would emerge as the man's hell bound slave, from the very bowels of the earth, like some troll or goblin or succubus now cemented to his will. For she knew that these lonely, abandoned hours, her subterranean, tomb like placement would work some change on her. She would emerge from her burial place transformed into something entirely new. The old Carly would be left behind to molder in her grave.

Then, finally, she heard what she thought was a car. Her heart leapt. All her reserve wilted away and she started whining and moaning and pleading with him to come free her. It took the longest time! What was he doing? What was taking so long?

And then she thought, maybe it's someone else, someone who had come into the woods to hunt or bird watch or something. Maybe some kids to drink and fuck or to smoke pot. They might not even see her. But he might see them and drive away rather than risk discovery. She tried to yell and scream as loud as she could, but only low moans came out. She shook her body from side to side, her shoulders butting up against the sides of the hole he had placed her in. She was beginning to turn hysterical. She knew that she should stop, but she couldn't. She yelled and yelled and yelled.

Something above her moved. The tent was being cleared of brush and branches. Someone was there! Who? Who?

When she felt his hands on her, she knew immediately who it was. It tempered her joy at liberation somewhat, but only a little. She hadn't really expected anybody else to come way out here. The top of the tent was pulled aside and she saw light. Her feet were freed and he let them down slowly. She moaned at the pain. He pulled her to her knees and then her feet. She could barely stand. She looked at him pleadingly, gratefully. He had come back! He had come back!

He had her sit down on the ground, her hand still bound behind her. She looked a wreck. She was trembling and her face was wet with tears. Well, he didn't have much time to commiserate with her. He quickly gathered up their stash and brought it over to the Marquee, putting most of it in the trunk. He kept some snacks and stuff to put in the passenger compartment. He folded up the tent. The girl watched him as if what he was doing was the most interesting thing she had ever seen.

When everything was ready, he went and got her. "She's not going to be happy," he thought. He let her pee and then removed her gag so that she could drink some water. She finished off almost a full 24 oz. bottle. When he presented the gag to her lips again, she frowned, but she opened them. He affixed it tightly behind her head. The trunk was still open. He dragged her over to it. She looked into it and whined. He couldn't help it. She was just too hot. He lifted her and put her in. He tied off her legs again to her wrists and slammed the trunk closed. He got back in the Merc, started it up and then they were on their way once more.

He skirted around Kansas City and headed southeast on a two laned county road. He didn't want to keep too direct a path south. He figured that they might be looking for him near Tulsa or Wichita, so he waited until he had gone about 30 miles east before he turned south again.

The snow was coming down heavier now and was starting to stick. The terrain was getting rougher too and they were mostly headed up. He crossed the Arkansas border at a small town called Gateway and headed up into the mountains. He knew that it was getting pretty cold out and that the girl in the trunk must be freezing. He was dog tired too. He needed to find a place to pull off the road. He passed through a small town called Bentonville and saw a sign for a place called Cave Springs. It sounded like a tourist place. He was right. He passed a few motels until he saw the one he wanted. It was set back off the road about 50 yards and had a number of little cabins. He pulled up and parked the car where it couldn't be seen from the motel office. He turned to the back seat.

"I'm getting a room," he said loudly so she could hear him through the back seat. "Just stay quiet for a little while longer. Then I'll get you something to eat and we can sleep. Just remember, if you fuck up, I'll kill you. And don't think I won't."

He went into the motel office and got them a cabin at the edge of the property like before. He had taken a quick glance at the license plate number before he went inside so that there would be no suspicions when he registered. He put down two names. Not stupid names like before. He used the name of the guy who owned the car, Peter Lindley, and his imaginary wife, Susan. He told the manager that she was asleep in the car.

He drove over to the cabin. He unlocked and opened the door. Then he made sure that so one was looking. It was about 4:30 in the afternoon. Due to the snow, it had started getting dark already. It wasn't coming down blizzard style yet, but it soon would and visibility was already poor. He had gotten off the road just in time.

He went around to the trunk and popped it open. The girl looked at him forlornly. He could tell that she was freezing. He undid her ankles and lifted her from the trunk. It was only about 15 feet to the door of the cabin and he practically carried her there. He brought her in, closed the door and put her on the bed. He didn't hog tie her, but merely clipped her ankles together. She just lay there on her belly while he brought in the rest of the things they would need from the car. He turned on the heat, pulled down the curtain to the one, large window near the door and then sat down on a chair by the small table near the kitchen area.

The room was much like the one they had had back in Wisconsin. The double bed was almost all the way up to the wall on the right side, leaving just enough room to get by and an old bedside table with a small lamp on it up by the headboard. It had a wooden frame with little posts on the corners in imitation of a more fanciful design. There were four pillows and the bed was covered with a red and white calico quilt. There was an extra blanket on the end of the bed.

The kitchen area was, like in the other place, to the left of the bed. It was a little bigger and had a real stove and kitchen sink. The fridge was a real stand up one too. The bathroom was off the kitchen. It shared a wall with the bed. It was clean, not very modern and had an old style tub with knobby feet on it. A curtain rod went around the tub and a shower had been hooked up. The tile and the bathtub were all white or, actually, kind of a grayish white due to their age. The curtain was orange and blue swirls. A matching orange and blue throw rug was on the floor.

The cabin was paneled wood, like the other place, but someone had whitewashed the paneling and covered it with lime green paint. It was not very attractive. Yellow linoleum covered the floor by the kitchen and a brown rug lay on the floor over by the table. The room was lit overhead by a roundish, frosted light fixture that covered two bright bulbs. There was a standing lamp by the left side of the bed.

He was watching the girl. Her long, bare legs were enticing. Her joined hands rested in the small of her back. Her face was turned away from him and all he could see was her now, stringy, blond hair. She would need to be cleaned up, he thought. And fed. And they needed some sleep. Not necessarily in that order.

He opened a can of Chef Boyardee ravioli, dumped it in a pot and put it on the stove on a low heat. Then he opened a can of beef barley soup he had gotten for the girl. He put that in a pot on a burner next to the ravioli. Then he went over to his captive.

Straddling her, he unclasped the hook in the back of her blue denim miniskirt and lowered the zipper. She did not react. He was able to easily draw it down her soft thighs and off her feet. Her pale rear mounds greeted him. He had been thinking about them all day. He ran his hands over them. They were as soft and firm as he remembered them. The end of the dildo was just protruding from the girl's rear star. "Later," he thought.

Placing his hand in her hair, he gripped it tightly and ordered the girl to sit up. She obeyed and gave him a tired, morose look. Ignoring her, he reached for her waist and began to draw the t-shirt she was wearing up her torso.

He pulled it up over her breasts and then her head and drew it down her arms to her conjoined hands. He pushed her face down on the bed again and unhooked her bracelets so that he could remove her t-shirt and then joined them again.

"That's better," he thought. It was better that she be naked, ready for use. And it was better that his eyes be able to take in her not inconsiderable charms. He had risked an awful lot in keeping her and he wanted to get all of his money's worth.

Carly had almost exactly the same thought. Not that it was better necessarily, but that she was now naked, ready for use. She knew that she should be showing the man more energy and cooperation; her value as a sexual partner had, after all, saved her life today. But she was just so tired and hungry and dispirited that she couldn't do any more than obey his commands and follow wherever his hands led her. The time in the woods under the tent in that hole he dug for her had been horrible. It hadn't been much better to travel in the trunk of the car for many hours. He could at least have let her put on her coat.

She winced when he took hold of her hair again and pulled her to her knees and then off of the bed. She moaned slightly from the pressure to her scalp, but cooperated as best she was able. He brought her over to one of the wooden chairs and sat her down in it. She remembered his standing orders and spread her legs widely and sat back the best she could, giving him a good display of her breasts and sex. He sat in the opposite chair, looking at her. His face was always hard to read. She knew that he had had many years, 12 of them, in which to learn how to hide his thoughts and control his emotions.

But she knew a look of desire when she saw one and she thanked her stars that there was one in his eyes.

Jack kept his eye on the girl. He lit a cigarette and opened a small bottle of Pepsi that he had bought. He took a deep, refreshing drink, keeping his eyes on the girl the whole time. He knew that she must be thirsty, but decided that she could wait. Her eyes were red rimmed and she had dark shadows under them. The leather shield of the gag still covered her mouth and he thought pleasantly of the prick like prong having been inside her all this time. It made him recall that she still had the stone egg inside her and he was tempted to turn it on to see how she would react, but he resisted the temptation. She was probably too tired to respond to it anyway.

He released a large cloud of bluish grey smoke, and then, putting the cigarette out in the ashtray, got up and stirred the soup and the ravioli. They were just about ready. He took a plate from the 5' tall, white metal cabinet next to the stove and brought it and the pot of ravioli to the table. After he spooned the steaming pasta onto the plate, he went into the cabinet again and brought out a large soup bowl. He put that on the table and poured the soup into it. He put the soup on the linoleum floor.

Carly watched him place the steaming bowl on the floor a few feet from her chair. The idea of humiliating herself again like that made her despondency plunge even deeper than it was. She knew that the purpose of it was to emphasize the difference in status between him and her, but he had already established that. Why did he have to be so cruel? She was ready to obey him in everything. Why make her eat like a dog?

She felt a tear flow down from her right eye. She blinked her eyes to try and stop the tears. She had done so much crying. It served no useful purpose other than to demean her. It certainly didn't influence her captor in any appreciable manner. She just wished she could stop.

He watched the girl's eyes shift from the bowl on the floor and back to him. He noted the tear in her eye. It was exactly the reaction that he wanted. If she got too used to eating like an animal, it would not have the same effect. That was the time you got rid of them, when you had driven out all pride and self respect. She was holding up pretty good given the circumstances.

He sat back down in the chair and then edged it closer to her. His knees were almost touching the edge of her seat. He placed his hands on her shoulders, rubbing hem softly and then let them drift down over her upper arms, across her chest and then down over her pleasantly inviting orbs. She shuddered just a little when he took hold of them. His eyes were boring into hers, weighing her reactions. It had been just about 24 hours since he had fucked her and it was important to reestablish the overriding paradigm of their relationship: she was his to use in any way he wanted. Her only role was to open such of her orifices as he desired to enter and to suffer his lust arousing caresses without complaint.

His large hands surrounded her ample orbs. He squeezed them gently and then firmer and firmer and firmer, until the mounds were compressed beneath his hands. She emitted a low whine from behind her gag and her eyes turned soft and pleading. He lifted them slightly, letting them rest in the palms of his hands like two little delicate creatures. Then he leaned over and subsumed her fat nipples into his mouth, each in its turn, suckling them, running his hot tongue over them, nipping at them softly with his teeth.

Carly squirmed in her seat. She didn't want the heat of the man's mouth on her teats, his insistent tongue, his suckling lips to initiate a burn in her loins, but they did. She remembered vividly the heights of irrationality he had driven her to yesterday, in a cabin much like this. She didn't know how long they would stay in this one, but the bed behind her loomed large in her mind as she was sure he would repeat yesterday's performance, entering her with his thick, remorseless cock, driving her to mindless ecstasy.

She had an image of her body dissolving into nothingness, fading away and leaving behind only the demeaning and confining instruments he had placed in and on her. If only she could do it, she thought. "Beam me up, Scotty!" she would call out. "A Romulan has captured me!" But she knew that it could not happen. She could only remain at the point in time and space in which she now found herself and suffer and bear the pleasures and humiliations he inflicted on her. She moaned as the suction of his lips on her breast caused an undeniable tugging in her womb.

Jack heard her moan and released her teat. He leaned back, smiling. She was a hot one all right. He took hold of her nipples between his thumbs and forefingers. He had reminded her of how her desires were enslaved to him. Now he would show her the other thing. He began to twist her flesh. He did it slowly, increasing the pressure incrementally. Her eyes expressed her, at first, concern, and then dismay. As his efforts began to twist and derange her teats, her eyes' expressions turned to panic and then misery.

She released a moan of another kind. "Mmmmmmm-mmmmmm! Mmmmmmmmmmmmmm!" Sweat broke out on her forehead. Her shoulders curled and her whole body tensed.

He released them. She gave out a sob and he pushed her shoulders back so that she was sitting straight. He took her breasts in his hands again and leaned over, reassuming her teats in his mouth, soothing them, suckling them gently, first one and then the other. Then he leaned back again and ran his hands down over her hips and along the tops of her widespread thighs. Back and forth he slid them, conveying to her his warmth and strength. He dropped his hands until they were on the tender insides, slipping them back and forth from her knees to the fulcrum of her thighs.

His cock was hard and needy. But he was enjoying his tantalizing caresses to the girl too much to seek fulfillment just yet. When he brought his hands up to the girl's face, she flinched and leaned back, fearful, apparently, of some new administration of suffering. But he was only releasing the buckle behind her head that held the gag so harshly in her mouth. He withdrew it slowly, letting the thick cock like protuberance rub across her lips. When it was out, he placed it on the table behind him. Her face was now entirely visible again and he was reminded of how beautiful it was. It was beauty crying out for despoliation. A tenderness which invited cruelty. A softness which required harshness. An opening, her mouth, which required filling.

He took hold of the hair at the back of her head, closing his fist around it tightly. The other hand wandered over her breasts, her chest, her belly and her thighs in a continuous, unhurried motion. Then he brought it up to her chin. He placed his fingers and thumb on opposite sides of her mouth and squeezed firmly. Her mouth sprang open. He leaned over, washed his tongue along and over her lips and then slipped it inside.

Her mouth was hot. She offered no resistance. Within a moment, her tongue was seeking his, flowing over and around it. Releasing her face, but keeping her hair tightly held in his other hand, he seized her breasts with his free hand, each in turn, squeezing them until she moaned. The sound reverberated into his mouth and echoed throughout his body. He let his hand drift south, over her belly until it found the entrance to her crevasse. He ran his finger up and down the slit between her engorging love lips. She had moistened and the finger was able to glide freely up and down, up and down, slipping easily into her. It was joined by a second and together they thrust back and forth, back and forth careful to abrade the ceiling of her chasm. They surrounded the stone egg that was inside her and slipped it out. There was a pause while he placed the device on the table and then the fingers returned, entering her gaping tunnel and sliding in and along the velvety passage. She moaned again. Her body seemed to melt. Her tongue became more feverish. When his fingers slipped free of her slit and centered themselves on her rigid love button, she moaned again, deeper this time.

Carly's mind had left her. Her rational mind that is. All that was left was the primordial mind that sought voraciously its own pleasure. She had no defense against the man's relentless and skillful assault. Her pussy was raging with need. When he placed his fingers on her stiffened nubbin, she thought that she might faint. All of the blood seemed to have left her brain and descended to fill her loins and her bursting breasts. The fingers went on and on and on, circling the tiny point of flesh, caressing it, agitating it, worrying it. She felt her orgasm building.

"Ohhhhhhhhhhhh, god," she thought madly. "I'm his slave! I'm his fuck slave! He owns me! Ohhhhhh, god! Make me come! Make me come! Make me come!"

And then she came. Her pussy throbbed and convulsed. She screamed her pleasure into her captor's mouth. He thrust his fingers in her pulsing crevasse and she could feel herself gripping tightly around them. Her heart was pounding in her chest. Her mind swirled as ecstasy poured through her veins. It went on and on and on.

Then, it slowed. His tongue, which had been dancing excitedly in her mouth, calmed. The thick digits which had filled her lower place withdrew. He leaned back. Her chest was rising and falling rapidly. He still had hold of the hair in the back of her head. He brushed his other hand over her breasts and belly, making her shudder. He kissed her once, twice, three times and then released her.

Jack took a good look at the girl. Her eyes were soft and unfocused. Her lips were still engorged and her chest was red and sweaty. Her nipples were taut and her hairless pussy glistened. What a stroke of luck she was! She was so fucking hot he couldn't wait to fuck her again. But he would wait. Being in the joint had taught him to delay his pleasures. Now that he had reestablished her place in the universe, that of being a toy for him to play with and use, they could move on.

He slid his chair back away from hers and pointed to the bowl of soup on the floor. It had cooled somewhat, but a thin waft of steam was still escaping from it. The girl looked at him and frowned. He reached out his hand angrily and took hold of her hair again. He lifted her from her chair and dragged her the three feet over to where the soup bowl sat. He reared his hand back and gave her one, two, three, sharp strokes of his powerful right hand on her buttocks, just below her bound hands. She shrieked and danced, but he held her hair firmly. He pushed her to her knees, lowered her torso and pushed her face into the soup. She gurgled and spluttered and then he raised it.

"Do you get the fucking message!" he asked her angrily.

"Yes! Yes! Please don't hurt me! Please!"

He struck her three more times on her rear. She howled with pain.

"Shut the fuck up and eat!" he yelled.

She was whining and sobbing, but as soon as he released her hair, she leaned her head over and began to lap up the soup. It was dripping off of her face and had spilled out onto the linoleum floor. He took the bowl away. "Lick that up!" he told her.

She sobbed, but obeyed. She licked the linoleum wherever the soup had spilled until it was all gone. Then she looked up at him miserably for approval. He went to the table and got a napkin. He wiped her face clean.

"Now, no more fucking around," he told her sternly. "You'll do what you're told when you're told, understand! And no more fucking talking! Got it!"

She nodded unhappily. He put the bowl of soup back down in front of her. He didn't have to tell her what to do. She spread her legs, leaned over and began to eat.

Jack went back to his seat. His anger had subsided. Now he meant to enjoy the sight of the girl eating like a little puppy. It had felt good to wallop her like that. He needed to be more careful about making noise though.

The last thing he wanted was some cop knocking on the door in response to a report of a domestic dispute. He would have to make sure she was wearing her gag from now on when he punished her. And because it felt so good doing it, he knew that there were definitely more punishments in her future.

The ravioli was okay. Not as good as he remembered it. He had eaten it a lot as a kid. In his house, with his drunken mother and his father who was never around and if he was, you wished he wasn't, if you didn't know how to open a can, you starved. And, later, when things got really bad, if you didn't know how to shoplift you didn't eat. Most of his early beefs had been shopliftings. That was until he learned that it was easier to force other kids to do it for you. You slapped some nerdy kid around and he would be your gofor for all eternity. Later, after he turned 14, it was easier just to do some housebreaking when he needed money. And then he learned how to deal coke. And after that he learned that as long as you had coke, you had pussy.

He shoveled down the rest of the ravioli. It still beat jailhouse food. He had bought some stuff to cook later that would be a lot better. The radio said it was going to snow until tomorrow afternoon. They would probably be here until at least tomorrow night, maybe until the next morning. For although he wanted to travel at night if he could, he didn't want to linger too long and tempt fate. He would not be able to really relax until he was in Mexico. So if he had to do some daytime driving he would.

The girl had finished her soup. She was kneeling on her heels expectantly. The bowl was completely licked clean. Her mien was dour. Well, that was to be expected.

It didn't matter. What mattered is her doing what she was told.

Jack pushed away his plate and turned his chair towards the girl. He motioned her over. She shuffled over on her knees, smart enough to know that she shouldn't get up. When she reached him, kneeling between his thighs, he cleaned her face of the remnants of her soup. He tossed the napkin on the table. He opened his fly and extracted his cock. She looked up at him. A momentary look of dismay crossed her face. Then she bent down and subsumed it between her lips.

His cock got hard right away. His libido was still well primed from when he had gotten her off. Her taut lips glided over his cock as it grew in her mouth. He leaned his head back, reveling in the moist heat she was delivering to him. He rested one of his hands on her head, not to guide her, he was leaving it all up to her, although he was ready to intervene if her enthusiasm flagged, but as a reminder to her of her duty to bring him maximum pleasure. She had given him an excellent blow job yesterday just before they left and he fully expected this one to measure up. If not, there was always the gag and the whip. He had saved the sapling branch he had used on her yesterday. No need to go out and get another one.

He needn't have worried. Carly was fully aware of the importance of doing her best. If she needed reminding, all she had to do was think of the sound of the bullet being loaded into the chamber of the man's pistol earlier today.

His cock was a thick presence in her mouth. While it was there, it was impossible to think of anything else. She rode her lips up and down it, giving it a gentle suckle on each upwards journey. She suckled its end like he had told her to do yesterday. She brought it all the way to the back of her mouth, poking it past the entrance to her throat, fighting off the urge to gag and choke. She swirled her tongue around it, varied the tempo of her strokes, licked her tongue over it up and down its length. The man was moaning softly. His hand was resting lightly on her head, an ever present reminder of his willingness to harm her if she flagged in her ministrations.

The soup sat warm in her belly. She had been famished, ravenously hungry. Despite having to eat it like an animal, it had felt good going down. His blows to her buttocks when she had hesitated to get down on her knees had stung viciously, but, even more, that had been a dreadful reminder of his strength and power. She was his prisoner and slave. He could snap her in two within a few seconds. He could deliver dehabilitating violence upon her at any moment. She was as surely trapped and powerless as a fly in a spider's web. The real world was just outside the door to the cabin, but it might as well have been in another universe, another dimension. She no longer had a place in it. For her, the whole universe was defined by the cabin's four walls and her god was the man whose prick was in her mouth. And she knew that she would suffer the wrath of heaven if she disappointed him.

His moans were growing louder, deeper and more resonant in his chest. The hand on her head had taken hold of her hair. His hips were thrusting upwards each time she brought his cock a downward stroke. She knew that he was ready to come and she redoubled her efforts. Forgoing all technique, she bought her head up and down rapidly, holding tightly to his thick stem with her lips, washing it with her energetic tongue. His grip on her hair grew tighter. His thrusts more determined. She sensed his body tensing. She heard him calling out, "Ohhhhhhh, yeaaaaaaah! Ohhhhhhhh, yeaaaaaaah! Ohhhhhhhhh, yeaaaaaaaaaah!"

And then he gave out a loud, anguished sounding grunt. He pushed his cock deeply into her mouth and began thrusting with his hips wildly. He had taken control of her head and was pumping it up and down rapidly. His cock was pulsing and jerking in her mouth. His spume filled it, running down her throat, all over her mouth and pouring out over her lips. He went on and on and, for a moment, she thought he might go on forever. But then he gave one more loud, needy grunt, thrust her face down deep into his lap, pushing his cock fully into her throat. He held it there for about 5 seconds, issued a deep sigh, and then relaxed.

It took a few moments more before he let her head up. She had started to choke and whine. That was okay. It added a piquant ending to the blow job. He had to give it to her, she was good. He wondered if her boyfriend, the guy in the picture in her wallet, got such great blowjobs from her or whether it was a product of her fear. Somehow, he doubted that the boyfriend had ever experienced her full devotion to his prick like he had. He didn't know what he was missing.

He finally let her head up off his cock. It slipped from her taut lips with a little 'pop!' Her eyes were downcast. There was a dollop of his cum on her lower lip. He drew it off with his finger and presented it to her. She looked at it for a second and then took his finger in her mouth, fastened her lips firmly to it and then drew it off. Then she looked up at him for approval. He smiled at her.

"Yeah," he thought. "You did a good job." With his free hand he reached out onto the table and retrieved her gag. He presented the business end to her mouth. She grimaced, but she opened her mouth readily. He slid the faux cock in and then buckled the straps together behind her head. "There you go," he thought. "There's your reward, a cock you can chew on all day long." Her eyes were dismal and sad. He laughed.

Still holding his hand in her hair, he got up from the chair. He pulled her along so that she was a couple feet away from it and then turned her towards the kitchen area. He released her hair and then pointed to a spot a few feet in front of her on the floor with the toe of his boot. "Put your forehead there," he told her. She looked at him quickly, and then away, and then she began to lower her torso towards the floor. She had to spread her long thighs widely in order to get low enough. Her hips raised and her back arched, she did it.

Carly listened as the man began to clean up from their meal. She heard the plate and bowl being washed and the two pots. It was funny that the position he had compelled her to assume was deeply humiliating, but somehow restful too. She just let her whole body relax. She tried to forget about the infernal presence in her mouth, forget about where she was and what she had just finished doing, forget about whatever abuse was still to come. She just took a deep breath and let all of her tensions run out.

She heard him drying the pots and pans and putting them away. She wondered whether his fastidiousness came from prison life or whether he had had it before. She thought that it was probably a trait he had had for a long time, from early in life. He seemed like such a measured, controlled man. If the news reports she had heard were accurate, he had led a big gang of motorcycle outlaws. You would have to be a fierce leader, tightly wrapped and very, very careful to have that much responsibility and power. She already knew how rigorous he was in controlling her, but for that one time when she had made a break for freedom. She knew it was not a mistake he would make again.

Jack put away the dishes and pots and pans. He liked the place nice and neat. He had always been a little crazy about that stuff, but 12 years in a tiny cell had made him more so. When your whole life was a 10 by 10 cell, you tended to make sure everything was put away exactly where it belonged so it did not get in the way. It was a habit born of necessity.

He turned and looked at the girl when he was finished. She looked so appealing and vulnerable like that. He was sure that if he lay down on the bed and went to sleep, she would be too terrified to move even if she heard him snoring. She trained well. It was the bright ones who trained the best. They figured out really early that blind, exact and immediate obedience was the best way to avoid pain. They more quickly became adjusted to the nuances of obedience, knowing your mind almost before you did, although never acting on that knowledge without per-mission. They learned too what tolerances you had for independent action on their part and never crossed that boundary. And they learned to fuck like Parisian whores, knowing that the more satisfied you were, the less likely you were to impose random violence upon them, generally speaking, that is.

He wanted to get cleaned up and then he wanted to sleep. He removed his shirt, tossed it next to the bed and then sat down on a kitchen chair to remove his boots. He stacked them neatly by the door and then pulled off his socks, letting them join his t-shirt by the bed. He then removed his pants, which he folded and put aside and then his shorts. He rummaged around in one of the bags and produced the 18" long chain he had bought yesterday. He stepped over to the girl, considered her for a moment and then leaned down and took hold of her hair. He guided her up to her knees and then to her feet and brought her into the bathroom.

Once inside, he looked around a little and then saw what he as looking for. The sink was stand alone supported by four steel legs. The drain pipe was exposed underneath it. He pushed the girl down to the floor on her knees near the sink and affixed one end of the chain to the ring at the back of her collar. The other end he wrapped around the drain pipe a few times and then brought the end to the girl's joined wrists behind her back. He fastened it off there. Then he joined her ankles together.

It had been a long time since he had taken a bath. He had been looking forward to one all day. He turned on the water, measuring carefully the temperature and then stepped back to let the tub fill up. He went out to the living area and retrieved a bar of fragrant soap he had bought today and one of the razors. He brought them into the bathroom and closed the door. The girl was right where he left her, of course. She was sitting on her heels and watching him carefully. He unwrapped the soap and put it in the soap dish.

When the tub was full, he turned off the water. There was steam rising from it. He put his foot over the side and tested the water. It was really hot, the way he liked it. He stepped in and brought his other foot up and immersed that as well. Then he slowly, ever so slowly lowered himself. He stopped for a moment when he got to his ass and balls. He dipped them down a bit to test it out. It was okay. He lowered himself the rest of the way, sighing from pleasure.

He leaned back. It felt soooooooo good! The heat just seemed to dissolve all the tension from his body. He closed his eyes. Ohhhhhhh, it was wonderful. His mind wandered. His body seemed to melt. He was thousands of miles away, at a beach somewhere. The sun was shining down on him. He could hear the waves as they struck the sand. Maybe a bird squawking in the distance. He had all day. There was nowhere he needed to be. Nothing in the world could hurt him. He was safe, removed from all hassle for all time.

He heard the rustle of a chain as the girl adjusted herself. He opened his eyes and looked at her. He was tempted to yell at her and wrench her nipple or some-thing so she would stay still, but he let it go. Nothing could bother him right now unless it was a bevy of state troopers busting in the door. And even if they knew where he was, in this weather it was unlikely to happen.

He continued to look at her. She had been a real find. She was beautiful. Her tits were just the right size for her torso and her skin was pure and white except for the fading red lines he had put there yesterday. Her eyes were bright and alert. It was too bad they had to meet this way. He knew though that if had met her years ago when he was on his run, he would have used and abused her for a few days, maybe a week or two at the most, and then handed her off to be put on the game. Now he was older and more appreciative of good pussy. Being without it for 12 years had something to do with it too. No, if they met now, or rather, once he got himself all set up again, he might even treat her decent to try and keep her around a while. He would call her by her name, which he still couldn't remember whether it was Carol or Crystal or something like that. He decided he would check later.

A feeling of contentedness came over him. He felt his eyes closing. He let it happen and in a moment, he was asleep.

Carly noticed right away that he was asleep. She saw his chest rising and falling rhythmically and his eyes closed. "Oh, god!" she thought. If only she could get free. But she couldn't even see the locks he had placed behind her when he fastened her to the drain pipe. It was frustrating to have the opportunity to run and not the ability. His eyes had turned on her like fire when she had shifted her weight and made the chain rattle against the pipe. If she moved now it would happen again and he would wake up. It was so disheartening! She had never conceived of what it would be like to be somebody's prisoner like this. She still didn't fully understand how it could happen. It was hard to believe. She wanted so desperately to be free that her whole body ached when she thought of it. But what chance did she have?

She had heard him undressing outside in the kitchen area while she pressed her forehead to the floor. She thought that he was going to take her to the bed and fuck her. She was surprised when he led her to the bathroom. She wished intently that he would just order her around rather than taking hold of her hair whenever he wanted her to move. It was so degrading. It was like she was a thing that he was moving from place to place, or an animal too stupid to understand human language. It made her feel so controlled and powerless, which was, she supposed, why he did it.

Once he had her chained in place and was preparing the tub, she couldn't help but look at his virile, strong, naked body. There were scars here and there, one big one down his left leg, a motorcycle accident perhaps. And his chest and back were covered with the cruel looking designs from the prison. He was like a creature that had ascended from hell. Strange looking, powerful, dangerous. He had been in hell, she thought. Prison must be like hell. You were surrounded by concrete and steel, men who were traitorous and evil, violent and cruel. Your life was ruled by men seemingly just as evil and unprincipled, the guards. You were condemned to year after years of grayness and coldness and darkness. She knew that he was evil long before they sent him to the prison, but how much more so had it made him? What would it be like for a normal person to be set down amidst him and his confreres? How could one survive? How could she survive?

Watching him step in the tub, so tall and broad and muscular, reiterated to Carly how small and powerless she was. He wasn't a man, he was a force of nature, a dark, evil one. How did one run from a tornado or a hurricane or an earthquake? You couldn't. You had to hunker down and hope it missed you, for if it didn't you were doomed, as she was. Doomed. She was doomed. She started to cry.

It was then she had made he chain rattle. When she saw him look at her, his eyes dark and piercing, a chasm opened in her belly. She knew she had sinned. She trembled as she saw him consider whether to punish her for her effrontery. When the moment passed, she gave out a sigh of relief.

She looked at the bathroom door. Outside it was freedom. She could tippy toe out, grab a blanket to wrap around her, undo the sliding bolt, open the door and run. He wouldn't know she was gone before it was too late. She would flag down a car, run to the motel office, awaken the other guests. "Shoot him! Shoot him! Kill him!" she would yell. For nothing less than his death would satisfy her. But she would want it to be painful and long. To make him suffer over a day, a week, a month. Maybe once they got him back to the prison they could string him up and flail the skin from his body, roast him over a fire, pull him limb from limb. And when he was dead, burn his body until it was dust and ash and then flush it down the dirtiest, scummiest toilet they could find. That would make her happy.

He groaned and then snorted, bringing Carly's attention back to him. His mouth was open. His face was covered with a day's worth of dark growth. But somehow it had lost most of its cruelty. He looked almost normal. Maybe even capable of kindness. It was a lie, though. She knew it. He was a beast from hell, come to consume her.

Jack's eyes sprung open. It took him a moment to understand where he was and he thrashed around in the tub. He saw the girl there looking at him with her forlorn eyes. "I'm in the tub," he thought. "I'm okay. I'm safe."

He dipped his hands in the water and brought some to his face. It helped him come to alertness. He looked at the girl again. He had to be careful. If she got away he would be screwed. He knew that for every moment he thought of how to confine her, she was spending 10 trying to figure out how to get free. He knew how it was. He had been a prisoner for 12 years. He had thought of freedom almost every moment of it. All of them did. It was like a poison spreading through your system, making you sicker and sicker the more you realized you would never escape. It was ironic that she was his prisoner now and was experiencing many of the things that he had felt. It was too bad for her. She wasn't that innocent anyway.

She was one of those normal people who paid their taxes and voted for people who built prisons and confined men there. She was as much his jailer as any of those screws back at the pen. Her and people like her. They deserved everything they got.

He got to his feet, took hold of the soap and worked up a lather. He soaped his body thoroughly. He washed his balls and cock especially well. He watched the girl watching him. She couldn't take her eyes off of him. When he was all soaped up, he did his legs and feet. Then he lowered himself back into the water, dipping even his head under, rinsing himself clean. He shampooed his hair. The tub had a removable shower head. He took it off and turned on the water and used it to rinse himself free of soap. He pulled out the plug and let the water begin flowing down the drain. Then he got out and began to dry himself.

He felt like a million bucks. It was just the thing that he needed. He went into the other room and lit himself a congratulatory smoke. He came back and, standing over the girl, his cock and balls practically in her face, gave himself a shave at the sink, the cigarette dangling from his lips. When that was done, he took a long leisurely piss in the toilet, tossed in his cigarette butt and flushed it. He brushed his teeth.

He turned to the girl. He wanted her clean too. He put the plug back into the drain and turned the water back on. He had purchased a special surprise when he was out. It was a bottle of bath oil. He poured a capful of it in.

Releasing her from the chain that had fastened her to the sink, he freed her ankles. He brought her over to the toilet and let her pee. After he wiped her, he made her stand while he put the lid down and made her sit on it.

He removed all of her bonds, the ankle and wrist bracelets and her collar. He had her stand up and turn around and he removed the prick like prong from her rear. Last, he removed her gag.

He took her by the wrist and led her to the tub. He tested it with his hand. It was hot, not as hot as he liked it. It would do for her. "Okay," he said to her, "get in."

Carly stepped carefully over the side of the tub, balancing herself with her hands on the lip and put both feet in. His hand was still in her hair. She lowered herself cautiously. It was hot, but not too hot. She felt it lap over her buttocks and thighs as she lowered herself into the water. He released his grip. The water had a layer of flowery smelling oil on it. As she submerged her body, she issued a sigh of contentment. After all she had been through, it felt like heaven.

She closed her eyes. She was conscious of the man hovering nearby, but she tried to blot him out. The hot water felt so good. And the bath oil smelled so pleasant. She could feel its oiliness on her skin. He let her lay there for a while. All of the tension and fear was oozing out of her body. She could have been home in her own bathroom, or at her parent's when she was a kid. She just wanted to lay there until she dissolved in the water. Then he could release the water and let her go down the drain. She didn't care as long as it meant full and complete loss of consciousness.

After a while, he told her to get up. Once she was standing, he took the soap and began washing her body. It was, at first, disturbing to have his huge, powerful hands on her after having achieved some freedom and relaxation in the water, but his touch was so surprisingly gentle and soft that she didn't really mind it. He soaped up his hands and washed her back and rear, taking time to make sure that her rear entrance was nice and clean. He washed her long legs. He made her turn around and washed her breasts and belly. He did her pussy too, careful to wash all around it and just inside. He had her lift her feet and he washed between her little toes. He washed her hands and each individual finger.

Once that was complete, hc had her get back into the water. He sank her head under the water and washed her hair. He sank her head again and then used some crème rinse on it. He brushed it out thoroughly. He gave her the soap and had her wash all her makeup off. Then he had her stand and he rinsed her with the shower head.

At this point, she assumed that he was going to have her get out, but he surprised her. He opened the drain and let out about half the water. Then he turned it on again so that it would fill up with hot. He poured in some more bath oil and had her lie back down. To her shock, he then left the room.

There was a little window next to the sink. Carly looked at it hopefully. It was very small. It would be tough to make it out through it, but she thought that she could do it. Then, she realized that as soon as she got the window open, he would come rushing in. He would beat her and punish her like he did the day before. The next time he thought about whether to kill her he might decide to do it. No, any escape attempt she made had to be assured of success. Otherwise, it wasn't worth it.

She lay back down in the water and closed her eyes again. If he was giving her this brief period of respite from him then she was going to take it. She dreamed of a bright, broad field covered with flowers. There were birds and big, fluffy clouds in a deep blue sky. She imagined herself flying up there, dodging in and out of the clouds, having the birds fluttering all around her. Randy was there. He was sitting next to her and he was smiling and laughing. He put out his hand and touched her arm. It felt so good. His grip got firmer and then she felt him pulling on it. She looked up and it was him, Blackjack, her captor, her tormentor. It was time to get out. She realized that she had fallen asleep and that he had come in silently. Her heart fell. She was back in reality, her dream dissipated.

He helped her out of the tub and pulled the drain. Using one of the big white towels that came with the room, he dried her off. She was dizzy and her body felt heavy, sleepy. He could do whatever he wanted to her. She was his prisoner. What was the use of resistance?

When she was dried, he gave her the toothbrush she had used the other day and made her clean her teeth. He made her use the toilet again. Then he sat her on the lid and began to reapply her bindings. She sat there listlessly as he surrounded her limbs with the leather bands. She did not flinch when he fastened her collar back around her neck. She rose dutifully, when he took hold of her arm and followed him as he led her from the bathroom and to the bed. She stood there as if in a daze while he pulled back the bedclothes and obeyed him without question when he told her to get in.

He went around the room tidying up a bit. He turned on the lamp on the bedside table and turned off the over head. She was half asleep when she felt him get into the bed.

She was on her side, facing him. She felt his hand on her shoulder, caressing it softly and then run down the length of her arm, over her hip and over her thigh. It came back and went down again and then repeated itself once more. His hand was warm and his touch was light. He was so large next to her. He made her feel tiny. He gently guided her to her back. She was so tired, she just wanted to push him away. His hand ran lightly over her breasts, fluttered over her belly and caressed the front of her thighs. She could feel the heat of his body next to her. His hand came back up and gently took hold of the breast nearest him. She sensed him leaning over. His mouth brushed on her teat. It kissed it. And then again. Then it surrounded it and the tongue washed over it ever so lightly. A warm feeling went through her body.

When the mouth began to suckle delicately on her teat, and his hand left her breast and washed over her belly and across the front of her thighs, she sighed. Her pussy felt that. It had begun to warm. She opened her eyes. She wanted to beg him to stop, to let her sleep, but his lips moved from her breast to her mouth. They brushed against her lips and she tasted his hot breath. A shudder went through her. He moved his body so that his chest was pressing against her breast, his left leg across her thigh. His tongue fluttered on her lips and then passed between them. A wave of warmth spread from the top of her head, down her neck and chest, past her breasts, over her belly and settled between her legs. She moaned and something went off inside her, triggered her need, sparked her yearning.

She felt his hand brush across her belly again. This time it descended over her loins and seized her pudenda. It was so hot and strong. She spread her free leg, her right one. A finger traced the line of her outer lips, slipped between them, gathered her moisture and settled on her now sensitized love button. She moaned and raised her knee. Her right hand, with a mind of its own, rose from her side and moved towards his body. It touched his shoulder and then slid down his arm to his hip and over the outside of his thigh. His tongue was swirling in her mouth. "Please stop. Please stop," her mind protested meekly.

Then, his body shifted. He was between her thighs. Her hands weakly tried to push him away, but her thighs spread wide open invitingly. His belly was matching hers. His cock probed at her entrance. "No! No!" she thought, but she was incapable of making any move to oppose it. She felt the bulbous head breach her pussy's inner lips and then the cock sliding home.

"Ohhhhhhhhhhhhhhhhh," she moaned.

He commenced long, desultory strokes. A lazy pleasure flooded her brain. They continued to kiss and her hands found their way to his wide hips. His skin felt so good, so hot. She could feel the outline of his muscles as he slowly moved back and forth between her legs. He was so strong! She knew she didn't want to be fucking him, but she couldn't marshal any energy to protest. What would be the point anyway? She had to let it happen, enjoy it, let the pleasure carry her away.

The abrasion of his thick meat along her canal was beginning to tell. Her hips shifted and her heart started to beat heavily. His hips were delivering a steady, rhythmic motion, slow but sure, not hurried or impassioned, just a man enjoying being sunk within a cunt. Her pussy gave her a twinge that made her eyes close and her back arch. Her heels dragged along the mattress. Her hands crossed over then man's broad, mighty back and clasped him to her. Her feet crossed the back of his shins, rubbing them and then ascended as far as they would go, up to his thighs, yearning to drive him further and further inside her at each stroke.

All of her body parts were in rebellion. She tried to catch herself. She pulled back her hands, drew her legs away, stilled her hips. She tried to still her tongue. His was circling it, toying with it, sliding to and fro over it. But her tongue wouldn't stop. It kept matching each one of his movements with one of its own. It was as if her pussy, with a mind of its own, was struggling with her for control of her body. The battleground was her tongue. And when her pussy proved that it was her tongue's master, all her other body parts, as if they had just been waiting to see who would win, erupted again into rebellion. Her arms clasped his body close. Her hips ground back at him, her legs again circled his, trying to force his thrusts deeper and deeper. Her pussy began to buzz as if in celebration of its victory.

Her whole body contracted. She felt like it was on the edge of a vast precipice. Her pussy was teetering on its lip. She tried to stop it from falling. Her mind reached out to grasp it. And then it was gone. Within a split second the rest of her body followed suit. She was plunging down, down, down into a pit that had no bottom. And then it came. Her pussy began a series of hard pulses that wracked her whole being. She tried to cry out, but all she could emit was a wavering, frenetic tone, "Ahhhhhhh-hhhhhhhhhh!"

The man's hips were slamming hers and hers were slamming back. His thrusts were long, intense and powerful. Her pussy grasped his meat hard and then released it again and again as if trying to coax its manly sauce from it. Her body was shuddering. She couldn't catch her breath. And then, just as her pussy's paroxysms of delight had begun to wane, the man grunted and groaned, his body clasped tightly around hers. He curled his hands under her thighs and drew them up. He pushed her knees against her breasts. He stroked her madly again and again. She felt like his cock had descended to the very depths of her being. The whole world was the area of contact between their organs. And her pussy exploded again. Their lips parted, unable to remain stationary amidst the onslaught of passion. She cried out. "Oh, yeah! Yeah! Fuck me! Fuck me!" He was grunting and groaning. She felt like he was going to split her in two. Wave after wave of excruciating pleasure passed through her.

And then, it began to fade. His thrusts slowed. Gradually, he lowered her thighs. He kissed her again, their tongues intertwining momentarily, and then he collapsed.

Carly's pussy still burned. It was fading, but the insides still vibrated. Her arms were still clasped around his back. "Oh, god, what has he done to me?" she thought. Her heart was beating madly and she was trying to recover her breath. In a split second, her revelry turned to self hatred and contempt. She had fucked him harder than she had ever fucked anyone. "I must be going mad," she thought miserably. "Look what he does to me!" She started to cry.

Jack couldn't move. He was exhausted. It had been one wonderful fuck! This girl was amazing. "I should never let her go," he thought. And then he heard her crying. "Yeah, go ahead and cry," he thought. "Your pussy belongs to me now, not you. I can make it do anything I want. You're just along for the ride!"

He forced himself up. His detumescing cock slipped from her slit. He rolled her over, pulled down her arms and connected her wrists behind her back. Rising from the bed, he went to the bathroom and recovered her gag and the black probe she had worn. After washing them both, he went back to the bed.

He took hold of her hair and forced her to her knees. When he proffered the penis like gag to her mouth, she did not resist, but accepted it docilely. He wrapped the belt from the probe around her waist. His pants were near the bed and he took from his pocket the tube of lubricant. Once he had the probe greased, he told her to put her forehead on the bed. She complied meekly and her rear rose to a proffering position. He pushed aside her rear cheeks with one hand, lined the fat, prick like probe up to her small, crinkled hole and then pressed it forward. The girl moaned and squealed as it entered her, but did not resist. He had her lean back while he ran the chains on either side of her mons and then up to the belt where he connected them. Then he pushed her back down to her belly and connected her ankles to each other. He turned out the light on the bedside table.

He could not forgo, in the dark, running his hand once more over her buttocks. They were smooth and warm. "What a prize," he thought. The girl was sobbing quietly. He pulled up the quilt and drew it over them both. Within a minute, he was asleep.

To be continued…